LEGEND OF THE LOST LEGEND

Look for more Goosebumps books
by R.L. Stine:
(see back of book for a complete listing)

Goosebumps®

LEGEND OF THE LOST LEGEND

R.L. STINE

AN
APPLE
PAPERBACK

SCHOLASTIC INC.
New York Toronto London Auckland Sydney

A PARACHUTE PRESS BOOK

ISBN 0-590-56884-1

12 11 10 9 8 7 6 5 4 3 2 1   6 7 8 9/9 0 1/0

Printed in the U.S.A.   40

First Scholastic printing, September 1996

1

Justin Clarke tugged his gloves under the sleeves of his heavy blue parka. Then he shielded his eyes with one hand and searched all around. "I don't see Dad," he told his sister, Marissa. "Do you?"

"I can't see *anything*!" Marissa cried, shouting over the wind. "All I can see is *ice*!"

The sled dogs barked and shook themselves, eager to start moving again.

Justin narrowed his eyes, squinting to the right, then the left. The ice stretched smooth and shiny, silvery under the bright sunlight.

In the distance, it darkened to blue. Darker. Darker. Until the blue ice appeared to melt into the sky. Justin couldn't see where the ice ended and the sky began.

"It's cold," Marissa murmured. A sharp gust of wind blew the parka hood off her red hair. She instantly reached up with both gloved hands and pulled it back in place.

Justin rubbed his stub of a nose. He pressed his

furry gloves against his frozen cheeks, trying to warm them.

The dogs tugged. Justin grabbed the handle of the dogsled to keep it from sliding away.

"What do we do now?" Marissa asked. Justin could hear a slight tremble in her voice. He knew his sister was as frightened as he was.

He stepped onto the sled runner. "Keep going, I guess. Keep going until we find Dad."

Marissa shook her head. She held her hood in place with both hands. "Maybe we should stay right here," she suggested. "If we stay here, it will be easier for Dad to find *us*."

Justin stared hard at her. Why does Marissa look so different? he wondered. Then he realized — the cold had made her freckles disappear!

"It's too cold to stay in one place," he said. "It will be warmer if we keep moving."

He helped her onto the back of the sled. At twelve, he was only a year older than Marissa. But he was big and athletic, and she was tiny and skinny.

The dogs grunted and impatiently pawed the silvery ice.

"I *hate* Antarctica!" Marissa wailed, grabbing the sled handle with both hands. "I hate everything about it. I can't even *spell* it!"

Uh-oh, thought Justin. Here she goes. Once Marissa started complaining, she never stopped.

"We'll be okay," he said quickly. "As soon as

2

we find Dad, everything will be okay. And we'll have some amazing adventures."

"I *hate* amazing adventures!" Marissa declared. "Almost as much as I hate Antarctica! I can't believe he brought us to this awful place — and then lost us!"

Justin gazed up at the sky. The sun had started to set. Wide streaks of golden light sparkled over the ice.

"We'll find Dad really soon," he told Marissa. "I know we will." He lowered the hood over his forehead. "Let's get going, okay? Before we freeze." He snapped the line and, in a deep voice, called out to the six dogs, *"Mush! Mush!"*

The dogs lowered their heads and moved forward with a burst of speed. The sled jerked hard as it started to slide.

"Whoooooaaa!"

Justin let out a startled shriek as he felt himself start to fall.

His gloved hands flew off the sled handle. He frantically groped for it.

Missed.

And fell off the sled. He fell hard onto his back on the ice.

"Ooooof!" He felt the breath whoosh from his lungs.

His arms and legs kicked the air, like a bug on its back.

He struggled to a sitting position. Blinking. The

ice shimmering all around him. Shimmering so brightly, he could barely see the sled as it sped away.

"Justin — I can't stop it!" Marissa's shrill shriek sounded tiny against the steady rush of cold wind.

"Marissa — !" He tried to call to her.

"I can't stop it! Help me! Help!" Her cry already so far away.

2

Justin leaped to his feet and started to run after the sled.

He fell again. Face first this time.

How can I run in snowshoes? he wondered. They're like wearing tennis rackets on my feet!

He had no choice. He jumped back up and started to run.

He had to catch the sled. He couldn't let Marissa face the cold and the endless ice on her own.

"I'm coming!" he shouted. "Marissa — I'm coming!"

He lowered his head against the onrushing wind. He dug the snowshoes into the snowy surface of the ice. One step. Then another. Then another.

Running hard, he raised his head and squinted into the distance. The sled was a dark blur against the glowing ice. A *tiny* blur.

"Marissa —!" he gasped. "Stop the sled! Pull the line! Pull it!"

But he knew she couldn't hear him.

His heart thudded in his chest. He felt a sharp stab of pain in his side. His legs ached from lifting the heavy snowshoes.

But he kept moving. He didn't slow down.

When he gazed up again, the sled appeared larger. Closer.

"Huh?" His cry sent a puff of white steam floating above his head.

Am I catching up? he asked himself.

Yes!

The sled appeared clearer now. Closer.

He could see Marissa, holding on with one hand, waving frantically to him with the other.

"How — how did you stop the sled?" he choked out as he staggered up to her.

Her blue eyes were wide with fear. Her chin trembled. "I didn't stop it," she told him.

"But —"

"It stopped itself," Marissa explained. "The dogs — they all stopped. I'm frightened, Justin. They stopped all by themselves." She pointed. "Look at them."

Justin turned to the dogs at the front of the sled. All six of them had their heads lowered, their backs arched. They all whimpered and shook, huddled together.

"Something is frightening them," Justin murmured. He felt a sudden chill of fear.

"They won't move," Marissa said. "They just

hunch together, whimpering. What are we going to do?"

Justin didn't reply. He stared past the sled. Past the frightened dogs.

He stared at an amazing sight.

A blue lake. Almost perfectly round, as if someone had carved it out of the ice. A pool of water reflecting the clear blue of the sky.

"Oh, wow!" Marissa gasped. She saw it too.

In the center of the small lake, they both saw a creature sitting on a large chunk of ice. It had its head lowered, staring back at them.

A sea lion.

A blue sea lion!

"It's the one Dad is looking for!" Justin cried. He stepped up beside his sister. They both stared in amazement at the magical creature.

"The only blue sea lion in the world," Marissa murmured. "A creature from a myth. No one even believes it is real."

Where is Dad? Justin wondered, not taking his eyes from the enormous blue animal. How can Dad be missing this?

He brought us all the way to Antarctica to search for this creature. And now he's lost — lost! — and Marissa and I are the only ones to see it.

"Do you think we can get closer to it?" Marissa asked. "Can we walk up to the edge of the water and see it better?"

Justin hesitated. "Dad said it has strange powers," he told his sister. "Maybe we should stay back here."

"But I want to see it better," she protested.

She started to step off the sled — then stopped.

They both heard the rumbling sound at the same time.

A deep rumble, low at first and then louder.

"Where is it coming from?" Marissa asked in a whisper, her eyes suddenly wide with fear.

"The sea lion?" Justin guessed. "Did it roar?"

No.

They heard it again. Louder this time. Like thunder.

Thunder . . . *beneath* them.

And this time the ground shook.

Justin heard a cracking sound. He looked down in time to see the ice start to break.

"Ohh!" A frightened cry escaped his throat. He grabbed for the back of the sled and pulled himself onto it.

"What is happening?" Marissa cried. She grasped the sled handle with both hands.

Another rumble of thunder beneath them.

The sled tilted and started to rock.

The sound of cracking ice drowned out the low rumble.

Ice cracked all around. The ground appeared to split open.

The blue sea lion, perched in the center of the small, round lake, stared back calmly at them.

A loud *crack* made the dogs howl.

The sled bobbed and tilted. Justin grasped the handle as tightly as he could.

He peered down. And saw that the ground holding them had broken away, broken free.

As the ice cracked, the lake opened up. Water rushed all around.

It's not a lake, Justin realized. It's a hidden *ocean* — under the ice!

"We–we're floating away!" Marissa shrieked.

The dogs howled, drowning out the sound of the cracking ice. Water rushed up over the sides of the sled. A strong current carried the sled away.

Justin and Marissa held on tightly, struggling to stay on the rocking, tilting sled.

The blue sea lion faded into the distance.

And they floated away, bobbing and swaying. Floating out to sea.

3

"What happens next, Dad?" I asked.

"Yeah. Don't stop there," Marissa begged. "You can't leave Justin and me on a chunk of ice, floating out into the ocean. Go on with the story."

I pulled the top of the sleeping bag up to my chin. Outside our tent, the fire flickered low. I could hear the chittering of insects all around us in the forest.

I peered out through the open tent flap. Too dark to see the trees. I could see a narrow patch of purple sky. No moon. No stars at all.

Is anything darker than a forest? I wondered.

We had a kerosene lantern inside the tent. It sent warm yellow light around us. But no heat.

Dad buttoned the top button of his sweater. It had been hot in the tent when we came in after dinner. But now a damp chill had fallen over us.

"That's all for tonight," Dad said, scratching his brown beard.

"But what happens next?" Marissa demanded. "Go on with the story, Dad. Please!"

"Yeah," I agreed. "Do we float out to sea? How do we get back? Do you show up and rescue Marissa and me?"

Dad shrugged his big shoulders. Under the woolly sweater, he looked like a big, brown bear. "I don't know," he replied. "I don't know what happens next."

He sighed and bent over his sleeping bag. He has a big stomach, and it's hard for him to bend over. He started to unfold the sleeping bag.

"I haven't thought of an ending to the story yet," Dad said softly. "Maybe I'll dream a good ending tonight."

Marissa and I both groaned. We hate it when Dad stops a story in the middle. He always leaves us in terrible danger. And sometimes we have to wait for days to find out if we survive.

Dad sat down on the tent floor. He groaned as he pulled off his boots. Then he struggled to squeeze into the sleeping bag.

"Good night," Marissa said, yawning. "I'm so tired."

I felt tired too. We'd trudged through the forest since early morning, cutting our own path through the trees, and rocks, and tangled weeds.

"Justin, do me a favor," Dad said. He pointed to the kerosene lantern. "Turn that off, okay?"

11

"No problem," I said.

I leaned forward. Reached for the lantern.

My hand bumped it. Knocked it on its side.

And in seconds, the tent was ablaze with orange and yellow flames.

4

I let out a sick cry and struggled to pull myself out of the sleeping bag.

Dad climbed to his feet first. I never saw him move so fast.

He picked up a section of the canvas tent floor and smothered the flames on the tent wall.

"Dad — sorry!" I managed to choke out. I finally struggled out of the sleeping bag.

Luckily, the flames had only caught on one wall. I have too good an imagination. I instantly pictured us surrounded by fire.

I guess I get my imagination from Dad. Sometimes it comes in handy. Sometimes it doesn't.

Now I was breathing hard, my whole body trembling. "Sorry," I repeated.

"That was close!" Marissa cried, shivering. "Justin is such a klutz!" She had scrambled to the tent flap, ready to run outside.

Dad shook his head. "It just burned a small

hole," he reported. "Here. I can cover it with this." He spread the section of canvas floor over the hole.

"This thing burns pretty fast," I murmured.

Dad grunted but didn't reply.

"I'd hate to be in the middle of the forest without a tent," Marissa declared. "Especially in *this* weird country."

"Everything is fine," Dad said softly, still fiddling with the tent wall. "But no thanks to either of you," he added sourly.

"Huh? What do you mean?" I demanded, straightening a leg of my pajama pants.

"You haven't been much help," Dad complained.

"What did *I* do?" Marissa asked shrilly. "I didn't try to burn the tent down."

"You wandered off and got lost this morning," Dad reminded her.

"I thought I saw a weird animal," Marissa replied.

"It was probably a squirrel," I chimed in. "Or her shadow."

"Give me a break, Justin," Marissa muttered.

"Then tonight you both refused to get firewood," Dad accused.

"We were tired," I explained.

"And we didn't know where to look," Marissa added.

"In a forest?" Dad cried. "You don't know where

to look for firewood *in a forest*? How about on the *ground*?"

Dad was getting steamed.

Maybe he's right, I thought. Maybe Marissa and I should try to be a little more helpful.

After all, this was a very important trip for Dad. And it was really great of him to bring us along.

My dad is Richard Clarke. Maybe you've heard of him. He's a very famous writer, storyteller, and story collector.

Dad travels all over the world, searching for stories. All kinds of stories. Then he puts them in books. He has published ten books of stories. And he goes all over the country, telling some of the stories he has hunted down.

He has been on a lot of exciting trips. But this one was special. He brought Marissa and me to Europe — to this forest in the tiny country of Brovania — because of a very special search.

Dad had kept the whole thing as a surprise. But he told us about it as we made our way through the forest that morning.

"We've come to Brovania to search for the Lost Legend," he explained. He pulled a large black beetle from his beard and tossed it away.

"The Lost Legend is a very old manuscript. It is said to be hidden away in a silver chest," Dad continued as we walked. "It hasn't been seen for five hundred years."

"Wow," Marissa murmured from far behind us.

She kept stopping to look at bugs and wildflowers. Dad and I had to keep waiting for her to catch up.

"What is the legend about?" I asked.

Dad shifted the heavy equipment pack on his back. "No one knows what the legend is about," he replied. "Because it has been lost for so long."

He used his machete to hack away a tall clump of weeds. Then we followed him through a narrow opening in the trees.

The trees were so thick and leafy overhead, little sunlight could get through. Even though it was still morning, the forest stretched as dark as night.

"If we find the Lost Legend, we'll be very lucky," Dad said. "It will change our lives."

"What do you mean?" I asked.

His expression turned solemn. "The ancient manuscript of the Lost Legend is worth a fortune," he replied. "The whole world is curious about it. The whole world wants to read it. Because no one knows who wrote it — or what it's about."

I thought about it all day as we twisted our way through the forest. What if *I'm* the one to find it? I asked myself.

What if I look down and see the silver chest? Hidden between two rocks, maybe. Or half-buried in the dirt with only part of its silver lid poking up.

Wouldn't that be cool? Wouldn't that be *awesome*?

I pictured how happy Dad would be. And I thought about how rich and famous I would be too. I'd be a hero. A real hero.

That's what I thought about all day.

But so far, I knew I hadn't been much of a hero. In fact, I nearly burned down the tent.

And Dad was already grumbling that Marissa and I hadn't been much help.

I'll be more helpful, I promised silently that night. I snuggled lower into the sleeping bag, trying to get warm.

On the other side of the tent, I could hear Dad snoring lightly. Dad can fall asleep in seconds. And he's such a sound sleeper, you practically have to hit him in the head to wake him up!

Marissa and I are not like Dad. It takes us *hours* to fall asleep. And the tiniest, tiniest sound wakes us up instantly.

So now I lay on my back in the sleeping bag, staring up at the dark ceiling of the tent. Trying to clear my mind. Trying not to think about anything.

Trying to fall asleep . . . asleep . . . asleep.

I had almost drifted off — when an animal howl cut through the silence.

An angry howl. A menacing howl.

So close!

Right outside the tent.

I jerked straight up. Wide awake. Breathing hard.

I knew this wasn't a storybook creature.

This creature was real.

5

The air in the tent felt cold against my hot skin. I realized that I was sweating.

I listened hard.

And heard a shuffling sound. A low growl. The crackle of heavy paws over the leafy forest ground.

My heart pounding, I slid the sleeping bag down. Started to crawl out of it.

"Oh!" I let out a whispered cry as someone pushed past me.

"Dad — ?"

No. I could still hear Dad's steady snores from across the tent.

I knew it would take more than a terrifying animal howl to wake Dad up!

"Marissa —" I whispered.

"Sssshh." She held a finger up to her mouth as she crawled toward the tent flap. "I heard it too."

I moved quickly beside her. We stopped in front of the closed flap.

"It's some kind of animal," Marissa whispered.

"Maybe it's a *werewolf*!" I whispered back.

There goes my wild imagination again.

But aren't werewolves supposed to live deep in the forests of Europe? I think that's where all the old werewolf movies took place. In a forest just like this one.

I heard another low growl.

I grabbed the tent flap and pulled it up. Cold air rushed in. A gust of wind ruffled my pajama shirt.

I peered out into the night. A mist had fallen over the small clearing where we had set up the tent. Pale moonlight shining through the mist turned everything a shade of blue.

"What *is* it?" Marissa whispered from close behind me. "Do you see it?"

I couldn't see any animal. Only swirls of blue mist.

"Get back inside," Marissa ordered.

I heard more shuffling sounds. A loud sniff.

"Hurry. Get back in," Marissa urged.

"Just wait," I whispered. I had to see what was out there. I had to see what was making those noises.

I shivered. The air felt heavy and damp.

Wisps of the blue fog seemed to cling to me. I took a step out of the tent. The ground sent a shock of cold up from my bare feet.

I held my breath and took another step.

20

And saw the creature.

A dog. A big dog, tall. Like a shepherd, only with long, white fur. The white fur shimmered like silver under the misty moonlight. The dog had his head lowered. He sniffed the ground.

As I stared at the animal, he raised his head and turned to me. And started to wag his tail.

I love dogs.

I've always loved dogs.

Without thinking, I reached out my arms. And I ran to pet him.

"No! *Don't!*" Marissa screamed.

6

Too late.

I knelt down and petted the fur on the big dog's back. It felt soft and thick. My hand touched leaves and small twigs tangled in the fur.

The dog's tail wagged furiously. I petted his head. He raised his eyes to me.

"Hey —!" I cried out. The dog had one brown eye, one blue.

"He might be a wolf!" Marissa called. I turned to see that she had taken only one step from the tent. She clung to the flap, ready to duck inside at any instant.

"He's not a wolf. He's a dog," I told her. I studied him again. "At least, I *think* he's not a wolf," I added. "I mean, he's too friendly to be a wolf."

I rubbed the top of his head. Then I scratched the thick, white fur on his chest. I pulled blades of dried grass and weeds from his fur.

The dog wagged his tail happily.

"What is he doing out here?" Marissa demanded

in a loud whisper. "Is he a wild dog? Justin — he might be dangerous."

The dog licked my hand.

"I don't think he's too dangerous," I told her.

"But maybe he's part of a pack," Marissa warned. She let go of the tent flap and took another step across the ground toward me. "Maybe the other wild dogs sent him out as a scout. Maybe there are a *hundred* of them!"

I climbed to my feet and glanced around. Squinting through the blue mist, I could see the tall, dark trees that circled the clearing. A half-moon floated low over the trees, shimmery through the fog.

I listened hard.

Silence.

"I think this guy is alone," I told my sister.

Marissa gazed down at the dog. "Remember that story Dad used to tell about the ghost dog?" she asked. "Remember? The dog used to appear outside someone's house. It was such a cute little dog. Very sweet and cuddly. It would tilt its head up toward the moon and let out an '*eeeh eeeh*' sound, as if it were laughing.

"The dog was so cute, people had to come out and pet it. And when they did, the dog would start to bark. It would call its ghost dog friends.

"The friends were mean and ugly. And they would circle the person, circle faster and faster. And then gobble the poor victim up. And the last

23

thing the victim would see was the cute, cuddly dog tilting back its head, laughing *'eeeh eeeh,'* laughing at the moon.

"Remember that story?" Marissa demanded.

"No, I don't," I told her. "I don't think that's one of Dad's stories. It isn't good enough. I think it's one of yours."

Marissa thinks she's a great storyteller like Dad. But her stories are pretty dumb.

Whoever heard of a laughing dog?

She took another step toward the dog and me. I shivered. The forest air was cold and damp, too cold to be out in pajamas and bare feet.

"If he's a wild dog, he could be dangerous," Marissa repeated.

"He seems gentle enough," I said. I petted his head again. And as my hand slid down the fur on the back of the dog's neck, I felt something hard.

At first I thought it was another dead leaf matted in his thick, white fur. I wrapped my hand around it.

Not a leaf. A collar. A leather dog collar.

"It's not a wild dog," I told my sister. "He has a collar. He must belong to someone."

"Maybe he ran away and got lost," Marissa said, kneeling beside the dog. "Maybe his owner is searching the forest for him."

"Maybe," I agreed. I tugged the collar up over the thick fur. The dog turned his head and licked my hand.

"Does it have an ID tag or a license?" Marissa asked.

"That's what I'm looking for," I replied. "Whoa. Hold on. There is something tucked under the collar."

I pulled out a folded-up wad of paper. Squinting in the dim light, I started to unfold it. "It's a note," I told Marissa.

"Maybe it has the owner's address or a phone number on it," she said.

I finished unfolding it and held the sheet of paper up close to my face to read it.

"Well? What does it say?" Marissa demanded.

I read the handwritten words silently to myself — and gasped in surprise.

"Justin — what does it say?" Marissa repeated.

7

Marissa tried to grab the note from my hand. But I swung it away from her.

"It's a very short note," I told her. I held it up again and read it out loud:

" 'I KNOW WHY YOU'RE HERE. FOLLOW SILVERDOG.' "

"Silverdog?" Marissa lowered her gaze to the dog. "Silverdog?"

His ears perked up.

"He knows his name," I said. I ran my eyes over the paper, trying to see if I had missed anything. But that's all there was. No name at the bottom. Nothing else.

Marissa took the note from me and read it for herself. " 'I KNOW WHY YOU'RE HERE,' " she repeated.

I shivered. The blue fog lowered around us. "We'd better show this to Dad," I said.

Marissa agreed. We turned and hurried to the

tent. I glanced back to make sure the dog wasn't leaving. Silverdog had walked over to a clump of tall weeds and was sniffing around them.

"Hurry," I whispered to Marissa.

We both made our way to Dad's sleeping bag. He was sound asleep on his back, making soft blowing sounds through his lips.

I dropped to my knees and leaned over him. "Dad? Dad?"

He didn't stir.

"Dad? Wake up! It's important! Dad?"

Marissa and I both shouted at him. But he's such a sound sleeper, he didn't hear us.

"Tickle his beard," Marissa suggested. "Sometimes that works."

I tickled his beard.

Nothing. He snored away.

I brought my face down to his ear. "Dad? Dad?"

I tried shaking him by the shoulders. But it was hard to get a good grip under the sleeping bag.

"Dad? Please! Wake up!" Marissa pleaded.

He let out a groan.

"Yes!" I cried. "Dad?"

He rolled onto his side. Sound asleep.

I turned and saw that Marissa had crawled back to the tent opening. She stared out. "The dog is heading toward the trees," she reported. "What should we do?"

"Get dressed," I urged. "Hurry."

We both pulled on the jeans and sweatshirts we'd been wearing. I got one hiking boot on, then discovered I had a knot in the other shoelace.

By the time I pulled the second boot on, Marissa was already back outside. "Where is Silverdog?" I asked, hurrying up beside her.

She pointed through the thickening fog. Clouds had rolled over the moon. The heavy darkness made it almost impossible to see.

But I spotted the big dog loping slowly toward the trees.

"He's leaving!" I gasped. "We have to follow him." I started jogging across the dirt.

Marissa hung back. "Not without Dad," she insisted. "We can't."

"But someone is trying to help us!" I cried. "Someone knows where the Lost Legend is. They sent the dog to bring us."

"It may be a trap," Marissa insisted. "Some kind of evil trick."

"But, Marissa —"

I searched through the fog. Where was the dog? I could barely see him. He had reached the trees on the far side of the clearing.

"Remember the story Dad tells about the forest imp?" Marissa asked. "The imp puts out a trail of flowers and candy in the forest. And when children follow the trail, it leads them into The Pit With No Bottom. And the kids fall and fall for the rest of their lives. Remember?"

"Marissa — please!" I begged. "No more stories. Silverdog is getting away."

"But — but —" she sputtered. "Dad wouldn't want us to go wandering off on our own in the forest. You *know* he wouldn't. We'll be in real trouble."

"What if we found the Lost Legend?" I replied. "Then what? Then we wouldn't be in trouble — *would* we!"

"No! No way!" Marissa protested, folding her arms over her chest. "We can't go. No way, Justin."

I sighed and shook my head. "I guess you're right," I said softly. "Let the dog go on its way. Let's get some sleep."

I put my hand on her shoulder and led her back to the tent.

8

"Are you *crazy?*" Marissa cried. She spun away from me. "We can't let the dog get away! It may lead us right to the Lost Legend!"

She grabbed my hand, gave me a hard tug, and started to run, pulling me across the clearing.

As I ran after her, I tried hard not to let her see the big smile on my face. I *knew* my little trick would work with Marissa. It always does.

If I ever really want to do something, all I have to say is, "Let's not do it."

Marissa always disagrees with me. Always.

That makes it very easy to get her to do what I want.

"Dad said we weren't being helpful," she murmured. "He was giving us a hard time because we wouldn't find firewood. What if we find the Lost Legend? Then we'll be helping him — big-time!"

"Big-time," I repeated.

I pictured Marissa and me handing Dad the silver chest containing the Lost Legend. I pictured the shock on Dad's face. Then I pictured his smile.

Then I pictured the three of us on the TV news shows. I imagined myself telling everyone how Marissa and I found the valuable old manuscript — without any help from Dad.

My boots clumped over the soft ground. I stopped when we reached the trees.

"There's just one problem," I told Marissa.

She spun around. "What's that?"

"Where's the dog?"

"Huh?" She turned back to the trees.

We both searched the darkness.

The dog had disappeared.

9

The fog clung to the dark trees. Clouds still covered the moon.

Marissa and I peered into the darkness, listening hard.

I sighed. I felt so disappointed. "I think our adventure is over before it even started," I murmured.

Wrong.

A loud bark made us both jump. "Hey —!" I cried out.

Silverdog barked again. He was calling us!

We stepped between the trees, following the sound.

My boots sank into the soft dirt. Under the tall trees, the sky grew even darker.

"Stick close together," Marissa pleaded. "It's so hard to see."

"We should have brought a flashlight," I replied. "We left in such a hurry, I didn't think —"

A loud crackling sound made me stop. The crisp thud of paws over dead leaves.

"This way," I urged Marissa. I turned toward the sound. "Silverdog is right up ahead."

I still couldn't see the dog. But I could hear his footsteps over the dry twigs and leaves of the forest floor.

The dog had turned to the left, following a narrow path through the trees. The ground beneath my boots became hard. We both raised our arms in front of our faces as we stepped through a thicket of brambles.

"Ouch!" I cried out as prickly thorns pierced through the sleeve of my sweatshirt.

"Where is that dog taking us?" Marissa asked shrilly. I knew she was trying to sound calm. But I could hear the fear creep into her voice.

"He's taking us to someone who wants to help us," I reminded her. "He's taking us to someone who is going to make us rich and famous.

"Ow!" I pulled a burr from my wrist.

I hoped I was right. I hoped that the note didn't lie. I hoped that the dog was taking us someplace nice.

The footsteps turned sharply up ahead. I couldn't see a path now. Actually, I couldn't see three feet in front of me!

We kept our arms in front of us, using them as shields. And we pushed our way through a thicket of tall weeds.

"He's speeding up," Marissa whispered.

She was right. I could hear the dog's footsteps moving more rapidly over the ground.

Marissa and I began jogging, eager to keep up. Over our own crunching footsteps, I could hear the dog breathing hard.

The flutter of wings — *many* wings, low overhead — made me duck.

"Were those birds?" Marissa cried. She swallowed hard. And then she added, "Or bats?"

I could still hear the fluttering, in the distance now. The sound sent a chill down my back.

So many flapping wings!

"They were birds," I told Marissa. "They had to be birds."

"Since when do birds fly like that at night?" she demanded.

I didn't answer. Instead, I listened for the dog's footsteps up ahead. They seemed to be slowing down.

We followed the sound through an opening between tall bushes. And stepped into a broad, grassy clearing.

As we made our way into the grass, the clouds floated away from the moon. Under the moonlight, dew-covered grass shimmered like diamonds.

I gazed up from the grass — and gasped in horror.

Marissa grabbed my arm. Her mouth dropped open in shock.

"I don't believe it!" I cried.

I stared at the creature standing a few yards up ahead of us.

Not the dog.

Not Silverdog.

A brown-and-black-spotted deer. A stag with antlers that curled up from his head and gleamed in the moonlight.

We had followed the wrong animal.

And now we were hopelessly lost.

10

The big deer stared at us. Then he turned and trotted across the grass, into the trees on the other side.

Frozen in shock, I watched him disappear. Then I turned to my sister. "We — we made a bad mistake," I managed to choke out. "I thought it was the dog. I really did."

"Let's not panic," Marissa said. She huddled close to me.

A gust of wind made the tall grass whisper and bend. I heard a low moaning sound from the trees behind us. I tried to ignore it.

"You're right. We won't panic," I agreed. But my legs were shaking, and my mouth suddenly felt as dry as cotton.

"We'll go back the way we came," Marissa said. "We didn't walk that far. It shouldn't be too hard to retrace our steps." She glanced around. "Which way did we come?"

I spun around. "That way?" I pointed. "No. That way? No . . ."

I wasn't sure.

"Maybe we should panic," I said.

"Why did we *do* this?" Marissa wailed. "Why were we so stupid?"

"We thought we were helping Dad," I reminded her.

"Now we may never see him again!" she cried.

I wanted to say something to calm her down. But the words caught in my throat.

"This forest goes on for miles and miles!" Marissa continued. "The whole country is probably forest. We'll never find *anyone* who can help us. We–we'll probably be eaten by bears or something before we ever get out."

"Don't say bears," I begged. "There aren't any bears in this forest — are there?"

I shuddered. Dad had told us too many stories that ended with children being eaten by bears. That seemed to be one of Dad's favorite endings.

It was never one of mine.

The wind bent the grass back the other way. In the far distance, I heard the flutter of wings once again.

And over the whisper of the wings, I heard another sound.

A dog bark?

Was I imagining it?

I listened hard. And heard it again. Yes!

I turned and saw the happy expression on Marissa's face. She heard it too. "It's Silverdog!" she cried. "He's calling us!"

"Let's go!" I exclaimed.

I heard another long series of barks. The dog was definitely calling us.

We spun around and ran toward the sound.

Ran back into the trees. Ran through the tall bushes. Leaped over fallen logs. Ran to the barking.

Ran.

Ran full speed.

Until the ground suddenly gave way.

A hole opened up beneath us.

And we started to fall.

"Nooooooo!" I let out a long, terrified wail. "It's The Pit With No Bottom!"

11

I landed hard on my elbows and knees.

"Ooof!" I let out a groan as my face hit wet dirt.

A bottom.

A very *hard* bottom.

I glanced over at Marissa. She was already climbing to her feet. She brushed dirt and dead leaves off the knees of her jeans.

"What did you yell?" she asked. "I couldn't hear you."

"Uh . . . nothing," I mumbled. "Just yelled."

I glanced up. Marissa and I had tumbled down a short, steep hill. We'd fallen maybe three or four feet.

Not exactly a bottomless pit.

I brushed myself off, hoping Marissa couldn't see how embarrassed I felt.

When we climbed back to the top, Silverdog was waiting for us. The dog raised his head and stared at us with his brown and blue eyes — as if to say, "What is your problem? Why can't you two jerks keep up with me?"

As soon as we joined him at the top of the hill, the big dog turned and loped off, wagging his furry white tail. Every few steps, he glanced back to make sure we were following.

I still felt kind of shaky from the fall. Even though it was such a short drop, I had banged my knees pretty hard. They still ached. My heart still raced.

Dad and his crazy stories, I thought, shaking my head. The Pit With No Bottom . . . why would I even *think* such a crazy thought?

Well . . . what could be crazier than following a big white dog through a Brovanian forest in the middle of the night?

Maybe Marissa and I will have a legend to tell our friends when we're finished, I thought. "The Legend of the Two Incredibly Stupid Kids."

Or, maybe we'll find the silver chest containing the Lost Legend — and be rich and famous and make Dad proud.

These were my thoughts as my sister and I followed Silverdog along a curving path through the forest. The dog loped easily between the trees and weeds. And we trotted behind him, eager not to lose him again.

After a few minutes, we stepped into a large patch of tall grass. Marissa and I stopped and watched Silverdog run across the grass, prancing, raising his legs high. He ran to a small cabin on the other side of the grass.

The cabin stood silvery gray under the moonlight. It had one narrow door and one square window under a slanted red roof.

A stone fireplace stood beside the cabin. Some kind of barbecue grill, I guessed. Beside the fireplace, I saw a low pile of firewood, neatly stacked.

I could see no lights on inside the cabin. No sign that anyone lived there.

Silverdog pranced up to the tiny building, pushed in the door with his snout, and disappeared inside.

Marissa and I hesitated at the edge of the clearing. We watched the cabin, waiting for someone to come out. The door remained half-open.

We took a few steps closer. "This is where he wanted to bring us," Marissa murmured, her eyes on the cabin door. "Silverdog sure seemed happy to get home. Did you see the way he strutted? Do you think the person who wants to help us is inside?"

"Only one way to find out," I replied.

"The cabin looks almost like a fairy-tale cabin," Marissa said. "Like a cabin in one of Dad's old stories." She laughed, a quiet dry laugh. "Maybe it's made out of cookies and candy."

"Yeah. Right." I rolled my eyes.

"Do you remember the story —?" she started.

"Please — no stories!" I begged. "Come on. Let's check out the place."

We stepped up to the cabin. The whole building was only a few feet taller than we were!

"Hello?" I called.

No answer.

"Anyone home?" I called, a little louder.

No answer.

I tried one more time. "Hello? Anyone in there?" I shouted, cupping my hands around my mouth.

I pushed open the door. Marissa followed me inside.

We found ourselves in a warm kitchen. Light from a candle on a small table flickered over the wall. I saw a crusty loaf of bread on the sink counter. A carving knife beside it.

I saw a big black pot simmering on a wood-burning stove. It sent a sweet, tangy aroma floating through the room.

I didn't have time to see anything else.

As I took one step into the small kitchen, a figure burst in from a back room.

A very large woman wearing a long, flowing, gray dress.

She had flashing, bright green eyes. Blond bangs fell across her forehead, and long braids hung down the sides of her round-cheeked face.

She wore a helmet over her head. A cone-shaped helmet with two horns poking up from the sides. Like a Viking from long ago. Or someone in an opera.

Her arms were big, with powerful muscles. She had sparkling rings on every finger. A round, jeweled medallion swung heavily over her chest.

She dove quickly past Marissa and me, her green eyes wild, her mouth twisted in an evil grin.

She slammed the cabin door shut.

Pressed her back against the door.

"I've *caught* you!" she shrieked. And tossed back her head in an ugly cackle of triumph.

12

Her cruel laugh ended in a cough. Her green eyes sparkled at us, reflecting the candlelight. She stared at us hungrily.

"Let us go!"

Those were the words I *wanted* to shout.

But when I opened my mouth, only a tiny squeak slipped out.

Marissa moved first. She dove for the door. I forced my rubbery legs into action, and followed close behind.

"Let us out!" I finally managed to scream. "You can't keep us here!"

The big woman's smile faded. "Take it easy, kids," she boomed. She had a loud, deep voice. "I was just kidding."

Marissa and I both gaped at her. "Excuse me?" I cried.

"Sorry. I have a bad sense of humor," the woman said. "I guess it comes from living out here in the middle of the forest. I can't resist a really mean joke."

I still didn't understand. "You mean you didn't lock us in?" I demanded in a trembling voice. "You haven't captured us?"

She shook her head. The horns on the helmet moved with her head. She suddenly reminded me of a large, gray bull.

"I haven't captured you. I sent Silverdog so that I could *help* you." She pointed toward the stove.

I saw that the big white dog had dropped down beside it. He lowered his head, licking a big front paw. But he kept his eyes on Marissa and me.

My sister and I stayed near the door. This woman was strange. And kind of terrifying.

She was so big and loud. And powerful-looking. And those green eyes flashed and danced wildly beneath the horned helmet.

Is she totally crazy? I wondered.

Did she really bring us here to help us?

"I know everything that happens in this forest," she said mysteriously. She raised the jeweled medallion close to her face and stared into it. "I have ways of seeing things. Nothing escapes me."

I glanced at Marissa. Her eyes were wide with fright. Her hand reached for the cabin door.

Back by the stove, Silverdog yawned. He lowered his head between his paws.

"What are your names?" the woman boomed. She let the heavy medallion drop back onto her chest. "My name is Ivanna." She narrowed her eyes at me. "Do you know what *Ivanna* means?"

I cleared my throat. "Uh . . . no," I replied.

"I don't, either!" the woman exclaimed. She tossed back her head in another cackling laugh. The medallion bounced on her chest. Her helmet nearly toppled off her blond hair.

Despite the warmth of the small kitchen, I shivered. We had walked so far through the cold forest. I couldn't shake off the chill.

"You two look half-frozen," Ivanna said, studying our faces. "I think I know what you need. Hot soup. Sit down." She motioned to a small wooden table with two chairs in the corner of the room.

Marissa and I hesitated. I didn't want to leave the door. I knew we both were still thinking of making a run for it.

"Our dad . . ." Marissa murmured. "He'll be looking for us. He might be here — any minute."

Ivanna stepped over to the stove. "Why didn't you bring him along?" she asked. She pulled down two bowls from a cabinet.

"We couldn't wake him up," I blurted out.

Marissa glared at me.

"A heavy sleeper, huh?" Ivanna had her back to us. She was ladling soup from the black pot into the two bowls.

I leaned close to Marissa. "If we want to escape, now is our chance," I whispered.

She turned to the door, then swung back. "I'm so cold," she whispered. "And the soup smells so good."

"Sit down," Ivanna ordered in her deep, booming voice.

I led the way to the small wooden table. Marissa and I sat down on the hard chairs.

Ivanna set the steaming bowls in front of us. Her green eyes lit up as she smiled. "Hot chicken noodle soup. It will warm you and get you ready for your test."

"Huh? Test?" I cried. "What test?"

"Eat. Eat," Ivanna ordered. "Warm yourselves." She stepped back to the stove.

I watched her bend to pet Silverdog's head. Then I raised the soup spoon to my mouth. Blew on it. And swallowed a mouthful.

Delicious.

And it felt so warm and soothing on my dry throat.

I took a few more spoonfuls. Then I glanced across the table. Marissa seemed to be enjoying it too.

I had raised a spoonful of noodles nearly to my mouth — when Ivanna spun toward us from the sink. Her eyes went wide. Her mouth dropped open.

She pointed at us with a trembling finger. "You — you haven't eaten any of it — *have* you?" she demanded.

"Huh?" Marissa and I both gasped.

"Whatever you do, don't eat it!" Ivanna cried. "I — I just remembered. It's *poison!*"

13

The spoon dropped from my hand and splashed into the bowl. I grabbed my stomach, waiting for the pain to begin.

I glanced over at Marissa — and saw her roll her eyes. "Another joke?" Marissa asked Ivanna.

"Another joke!" Ivanna confessed gleefully. Once again, she roared with laughter.

I swallowed hard. Why didn't I guess it was another one of the woman's mean jokes? I hate it when Marissa catches on to things before I do!

"I knew it all along," I muttered.

Ivanna stepped up to the table, the medallion bouncing as she walked. "The soup isn't poison. But don't eat it yet," she instructed. "I want to read the noodles."

"Excuse me?" I replied.

She leaned over my bowl, bringing her face so close that the steam misted her cheeks. "Chicken soup noodles foretell your fate," she whispered mysteriously.

She studied the noodles in my bowl. Then she studied Marissa's. "Hmmmm. Hmmmm," she kept repeating. "Yes. Hmmmm hmmmm."

Finally, she stood up and crossed her powerful arms over her chest. Her cheeks were red from the hot steam off the soup.

"Eat. Eat your soup now," she instructed. "Before it gets cold."

"What did you see?" I asked. "In the noodles. What did they tell you?"

Her expression turned solemn. "You must take the test in the morning," she replied. "I was right. I know why you have come to the forest. I know what you seek."

She straightened the helmet on her head. "I can help you. I can help you find it. But first you must take the test."

"Uh . . . what kind of test?" I asked.

Her eyes flashed. "A *survival* test," she replied.

I swallowed hard. "I was afraid of that," I muttered.

"What if we don't *want* to take your survival test?" Marissa demanded.

"Then you will *never* find the silver chest!" Ivanna declared heatedly.

I gasped. "Wow! You *do* know what we're looking for!" I exclaimed.

She nodded. "I know everything in this forest."

"But — but we need our dad!" Marissa stammered.

Ivanna shook her head. "There is no time. You will take the test in his place. Do not worry. It is not a difficult test. If you stay alive."

"Huh? If we *stay alive*? Is that one of your jokes?" I asked weakly.

"No," Ivanna replied, shaking her head. "No joke. I never joke about the test in the Fantasy Forest."

I was holding the soup spoon. But I let it fall to the table. "Fantasy Forest? Where's that? What is it?"

Ivanna opened her mouth to answer. But before she could say a word, the cabin door burst open.

I felt a blast of cold air.

And then a wild creature, covered in black fur, scrabbled into the room on all fours. Snarling, it cast its bulging black eyes around the room.

Then it snapped its jagged teeth — and, with a hoarse growl, leaped to attack me.

14

I uttered a scream — and tried to dodge out of the way.

My chair fell, and I fell with it.

The chair clattered noisily onto the floorboards. I landed on my side.

I tried to roll away. But the snarling creature sank its teeth into my leg.

"Owwww!" I shrieked.

Over my cry, I heard Ivanna's booming shouts: "Down, Luka! Get down! Off, Luka! Get off!"

The wild creature gurgled. It let go of my leg. And backed away, breathing hard.

As I scrambled to my feet, I stared at the panting creature. It had a man's face. Hunched on its hind legs, it looked almost human. Except that it was covered with thick, black fur.

"Get back, Luka!" Ivanna screamed. "Back!"

The creature obediently inched back.

"Don't be scared of Luka," Ivanna said, turning to me. "He's a good boy."

"What — what *is* he?" I cried, rubbing my leg.

"I'm not sure," Ivanna replied, grinning at the furry thing.

Luka hopped up and down, grinning, making grunting sounds.

"He was brought up by wolves," Ivanna said. "But he's a good boy. Aren't you, Luka?"

Luka nodded. His tongue hung out of his open mouth. He panted like a dog.

Ivanna petted his long, shaggy hair.

He broke away from her and charged at me again. He sniffed my sweatshirt and jeans. Then he crawled under the table and sniffed Marissa's hiking boots.

"Get away, Luka!" Ivanna ordered. "Off! Off!" She turned to me. "He's a good boy. He's just nosy. He'll calm down — once he gets to know you."

"Gets to know us?" Marissa demanded, watching Luka scurry over to Silverdog by the stove.

"Luka will be a big help to you when you enter the Fantasy Forest," Ivanna said with a smile.

"He's coming with us?" I cried.

Ivanna nodded. "He will be your guide. And he will protect you." Her expression turned solemn. Then she added softly, "You need all the help you can get."

We finished our soup quickly. Silverdog and Luka watched us from beside the stove.

When we finished, Ivanna led us to a small back room. The room was bare except for two cots.

"You will sleep here," she said sternly.

"But our dad —" Marissa started.

Ivanna raised a hand to silence her. "You want to find the silver chest — don't you? You want to surprise your father and make him proud — don't you?"

Marissa and I nodded.

"Then you will take the test. If you pass it, I will tell you how to find the chest."

She dropped a coarse wool blanket onto each cot. "Sleep quickly," she instructed. "The test begins first thing in the morning."

I awoke slowly. Stretched. Turned and reached to push the blanket off me.

No blanket.

Had I kicked it onto the floor?

I blinked several times, trying to clear the sleep from my eyes.

How long had I slept?

Sunlight streamed all around.

Yawning, I sat up. Started to climb off the cot.

But the cot had disappeared, too.

"Hey — !" I cried out when I realized the cabin had also disappeared.

"Where am I?"

I was sitting on the grass, fully dressed. I blinked, waiting for my eyes to adjust to the bright morning sunlight. The grass still shimmered wetly from the morning dew.

I stood up. My mouth dry. Feeling stunned. Nothing but forest all around.

My mind whirled. Ivanna had said the test would begin first thing in the morning.

Had it already begun? Was I in the Fantasy Forest?

Had the test begun *before* I awoke?

Rubbing my eyes, I turned to Marissa. "Where are we?" I asked, my voice still hoarse from sleep. I cleared my throat. "Do you think —"

I stopped with a gasp when I realized Marissa wasn't there.

I was alone.

Alone in the middle of the forest.

"Marissa — ?" I called, feeling the panic tighten my chest. Where *was* she?

Where was *I*?

"Marissa — ? Marissa — ?"

15

"Marissa — ?"

My voice cracked. My throat tightened.

I heard a low growl from the trees. The thud and crackle of heavy animal footsteps.

I turned to the sound. And watched Luka come hopping out of the forest. He stood on his two feet like a man. But he hopped like a rabbit. Scratching the thick fur on one leg, he grinned at me as he came near.

I didn't grin back. "Where is Marissa?" I demanded. "Where is my sister?"

He tilted his head and stared at me, confused.

"Marissa!" I screamed at him. "Where is Marissa?"

"Over here!"

I jumped when her voice leaped out at me. "Where are you?" I called.

I saw a flash of her red hair. Then she poked her head out from behind a wide, leafy bush.

"Over here," she repeated. "You were still asleep. So I thought I'd explore."

"You scared me to death!" I admitted. I began trotting through the tall grass and weeds, eager to join her. "Where are we?" I demanded. "What happened to Ivanna's cabin?"

Marissa shrugged. "Beats me. I woke up — and here we were."

Behind us, Luka growled.

I turned and saw him pawing the dirt, like a dog. "Do you think he's part human?" I whispered to Marissa.

She didn't seem to hear me. She pointed to a spot between two trees. "I found a path over there. Do you think we're supposed to follow it?"

"I don't know *what* we're supposed to do," I replied shrilly. "Did Ivanna ever explain the test? No. Did she ever tell us the rules? No. Did she ever tell us what we're supposed to do to *pass* the test? No."

Marissa's eyes narrowed in fear. "I think we're supposed to stay alive," she said softly. "I think that's how we pass the test."

"But where do we go? What do we do?" I cried. I could feel myself start to lose control. I felt angry and frightened and confused — all at the same time.

Luka uttered another growl. He stopped digging up the dirt and came staggering over to us, standing up like a human.

If he shaved off all the fur, put on some clothes, and got a haircut, he'd look like a young man, I thought. As I stared at him, he started to wave and point.

"What is he doing?" I asked Marissa.

She stepped up beside me and stared at him too.

Luka grunted excitedly. He waved a furry hand at us and jabbed his other hand toward the trees.

"I think he wants us to follow him," I said.

"Yes," Marissa agreed. "Remember — Ivanna said he would be our guide."

Grunting and waving, Luka headed for the trees.

I held back. "Can we trust him?" I asked.

Marissa shrugged. "Do we have a choice?"

Luka stepped onto a path that led through the forest. The path curved behind a clump of tall, yellow-leafed bushes. I saw his head bobbing above the bushes. Then he disappeared.

"Hurry!" I tugged my sister's arm. "We'd better not let him get out of sight."

I glanced down and saw two black backpacks on the grass. I bent down, grabbed one, and unzipped it. Empty.

I handed the other backpack to Marissa. "Ivanna must have left these for us," I told her. "They're empty. But I guess we should take them."

We pulled the backpacks onto our backs. Then

we jogged to the path and hurried to catch up with the bouncing, hopping Luka.

He stopped to sniff a weed. Then he continued shuffling along the path.

We followed close behind. Two or three times, he turned back to make sure we were following.

The path curved between prickly weeds and tall reeds. We passed a small, round pond that reflected the blue sky. The air became warmer and wet. The back of my neck felt hot and prickly.

We entered a cluster of trees with smooth, white trunks. The trees grew close together. The smooth bark of the trunks felt cool against my hot hands.

"Where is he taking us?" Marissa whispered.

I didn't answer her. I didn't know. I only knew that Luka was leading us deeper and deeper into this forest.

We squeezed our way through the white-trunked trees. And came out in a large, grassy clearing. Small gray rocks poked up from the grass. The slender white trees formed a circle around the clearing.

My boots crunched over the ground as I followed Luka across the grass. I looked down to see what made the crunching sound.

And discovered that the ground was covered with large brown nuts.

I picked one up. "Check this out," I called to Marissa. I turned and saw that she had picked up two of them. "They must have fallen off the white trees," I said.

"They look like walnuts. But they're bigger than eggs!" she declared. "I never saw walnuts this big!"

"They feel so hot!" I exclaimed. I glanced up at the sky. "I guess it's from the sun beating down on them."

"Hey — ! Whoa!"

Marissa's cry made me look up.

I saw a gray creature scamper across the clearing.

At first I thought it was a dog or a very large cat. Then I realized it was a squirrel. It carried one of the large nuts in its front paws. And it hopped quickly toward the trees, its bushy gray tail floating behind it like a pennant.

I turned as Luka let out a hoarse cry.

I saw him stand straight up. I saw his eyes go wide with excitement.

He let out another cry. Leaned forward. Reached out both hands.

And started to chase after the squirrel.

The squirrel saw Luka coming. It dropped the nut and took off at full speed into the white trees.

Luka dropped to all fours and galloped after it.

"No, Luka — come back!" Marissa shouted.

"Come back! Come back!" we both called. "Luka — come back!"

16

Marissa and I both let out worried cries. Then we took off after Luka, into the clump of trees.

"Luka — ! Hey, Luka!" I called. My voice bounced off the trees. It echoed all around me.

"Luka — ! Hey, Luka!"

The cry repeated and repeated, echoing loudly.

I could hear his growl up ahead. And I could hear him thrashing his way through the trees as he chased the fat squirrel.

"Luka — come back!" Marissa's cry echoed all around the forest, too.

As we called after him, it sounded as if there were *dozens* of us in the forest, all chasing after him, all frantically calling for him to stop chasing that squirrel and come back to us.

"Whoa!" I cried out as I tried to slip through the narrow space between two white tree trunks — and my backpack caught between the trees.

"Ow!"

It snapped me back. I staggered and nearly fell.
Mister Klutz. For a change.

"Luka! Hey — Luka!" I could hear Marissa's cry up ahead of me now.

I tried to slip through the trees again, and the backpack caught again. I pulled it free and found another, wider opening.

A few seconds later, I caught up with my sister. She had stopped running. She leaned against a tree trunk, breathing hard.

"Where is he?" I cried. "Do you see him? Where did he go?"

"I — I lost him," Marissa replied breathlessly. "I don't even hear him anymore."

I listened hard. The forest was silent now. No footsteps. No growls. The leaves above us brushed together, making a soft, whispering sound.

"But how could he run away?" I cried. "He's supposed to be our guide!"

"I think he really wanted to catch that squirrel," Marissa said quietly.

"But — but —" I sputtered. "He can't just run away and leave us all by ourselves here."

Marissa sighed. "I think he just did."

"We have to find him!" I cried. "Come on. We have to keep going. We can't let him —"

Marissa shook her head. "How can we find him, Justin? Which way should we go?"

"We'll follow his footprints," I replied. I lowered my gaze to the ground. A thick carpet of brown leaves spread over the dirt.

No footprints.

"I think he was heading that way," I said, pointing to the trees.

Marissa shook her head. "I don't think so." She pushed herself away from the tree trunk. "He's gone, Justin."

I spun around, frantically searching for him. For any sign of him.

"Hey — what's that?" Marissa called.

"Huh?" I turned back to her.

"In your back pocket," she said, pointing. "What is it?"

Confused, I reached into the back pocket of my jeans — and pulled out a folded-up sheet of paper. My hands were sweaty and stuck to the paper. But I unfolded it quickly.

"It's some kind of a note," I told Marissa. "In a tiny handwriting."

"Well, *read* it!" she cried.

My eyes slid to the bottom of the page. "It– it's from Ivanna," I stammered excitedly.

"What does it say?" Marissa demanded impatiently.

I steadied the page between both my hands and read the note out loud to both of us:

"DEAR KIDS,
       KEEP LUKA WITH YOU, AND

YOU WILL PASS THE TEST. DO
NOT LET HIM OUT OF YOUR
SIGHT. BE CAREFUL NOT TO
LOSE HIM — OR YOU ARE
DOOMED."

17

Marissa and I made our way slowly back to the clearing. The grass swayed under a soft breeze. Our boots crunched over the large nuts in the grass.

I still held Ivanna's note in my hand. I glanced over it one more time, hoping it didn't say what it said. Then I angrily balled it up and tossed it away.

Marissa trudged along beside me. The sun beat down on us. We were both sweating.

"Maybe if we wait here, Luka will come back," Marissa said.

"He isn't coming back," I groaned. "He is probably miles away, still chasing after that squirrel."

"Then what do we do next?" Marissa demanded. "How do we pass the test?"

I let out an unhappy sigh. "We *can't* pass the test. You heard what the note said. We're doomed."

"Well, we can *try*," she insisted. She started across the clearing. I followed her.

We had taken six or seven steps when I heard a startling sound. A loud *snap*, like a pencil being broken in two.

Then a *crack* — soft at first, and then louder.

I stopped and whirled around. I expected to see Luka come bounding out of the forest.

But I saw only the tall, white trees. No one there.

I heard another sharp *snap*. Then another. And another.

And then I heard cracking all around.

The earth is cracking open!

That was my first thought. I pictured the ground splitting apart. A dark hole opening up. And Marissa and me falling, falling down into it.

The Pit With No Bottom!

I wished Dad had never told us that story!

Now Marissa grabbed my shoulder and pointed down. "Justin — look!"

I gazed down. The ground hadn't split open. But the snapping and cracking echoed all around.

Louder. Louder.

"Ohh!" I let out a frightened moan as I realized to my horror that the grass was moving.

I could feel it move under my feet.

"What's *happening*?" Marissa cried, still holding on to me. "That sound — !"

The cracking grew louder, rising up from the

ground. Now it sounded as if all the trees were cracking apart.

The grass swayed and bent.

"It's — the nuts!" I cried to Marissa. "Look! They're all cracking open!"

I covered my ears against the sound.

And stared at the nuts, bouncing and trembling all around our feet.

Cracking open. Splitting apart.

Hundreds and hundreds of them. The whole clearing. The ground shaking as they all cracked apart.

Cracked into pieces. Crumbled around us.

We stared in amazement at the cracking nuts. And then, Marissa and I both screamed in shock when we saw what came climbing out.

18

Staring down as a nut split open, I saw gnashing teeth. Tiny black eyes. A twitching black nose.

The creature pushed itself up. I saw spindly front legs.

A slender body of gray fur.

And those teeth. Snapping. Gnashing.

"A mouse!" I choked out.

"Hundreds of them!" Marissa cried.

The nuts were splitting apart. All across the clearing. So many of them, it made the grass quiver and the ground appear to shake.

I stood frozen in place, watching mice hatch around my feet. They pushed out slowly, poking their heads out first. Sniffing the air. Trying out their pointy teeth.

The nuts rocked onto their sides. Cracked apart. Gray bodies slithered out. Sticklike back legs kicked their way out from the empty shells.

"They're not nuts — they're eggs!" Marissa wailed.

"But mice don't come from eggs!" I protested.

Marissa raised her eyes to me, her face twisted in shock. "I guess no one told these mice!"

A mouse scampered over my boots. Mice were scurrying through the tall grass, making the grass whisper.

Another gray body slithered over my boots.

"Let's get *out* of here!" I cried to Marissa. I grabbed her arm and started to pull.

But so many mice scampered over the grass, so many gray bodies slithered at our feet — we couldn't move.

Shrill squeaks rose up from the grass as the creatures found their voices. "*Eee eee eee eee!*" The sound surrounded us. Grew louder, louder. Until it drowned out the whisper of the grass. Until it forced Marissa and me to cover our ears.

"*Eee eee eee eee!*"

"We have to *run!*" I shouted.

"But the ground is covered!" Marissa shrieked. "If we run —"

"YOWWWWW!" I let out a cry as I felt a mouse drop inside my hiking boot. Its tiny feet scratched through my wool socks.

I bent down to pull it out — and saw two more mice clinging by their teeth to my pants cuff.

"Hey —" I tried to bat them away.

Lost my balance.

Fell to my knees.

Justin the Super Klutz strikes again.

69

Mice scurried over my hands. I felt one climb up my sweatshirt sleeve, onto my back.

"Hellllp!" Marissa and I both cried out at the same time.

I turned and saw her bent over, hands raised, struggling to pull two mice from her hair.

Another mouse chewed the bottom of her sweatshirt. Two more mice climbed a leg of her jeans. Mice clung to her backpack.

"Helllp me! Ohhhh — helllp!"

Still on my knees, I struggled to push myself up. But a mouse slithered under my sweatshirt. I felt its prickly feet move across my chest. Then I felt a sharp stab of pain in the middle of my back.

Did it *bite* me?

Mice jumped onto my shoulders. Crawled over the back of my neck. Swarmed over my backpack.

Swinging both hands wildly, I tried to brush them off me.

But there were too many of them.

Squeaking. Snapping. Clinging to my clothes. My wrists. My hair.

"Helllllp! Hellllp!"

I pulled a mouse from my ear. And tossed it across the grass.

I could feel a bunch of them crawling over my bare skin under my sweatshirt. Another sharp bite made me cry out — and I dropped facedown onto the grass — onto more mice!

I tried to swat the mice away. Tried to swat them and push them and grab them and tug them off me.

But there were too many. Way too many.

I turned and saw them swarming over Marissa. She cried out as she spun around, swinging her arms. Trying to shake the mice off.

I wanted to help her. But I couldn't get up.

My whole body tingled and itched.

The squeaking, chattering mice swarmed over me, holding me down. Prickling me, scratching me, biting me — until I couldn't move, couldn't breathe.

19

"Off! Get off!" I managed to cry.

I swiped at my face, slapping two mice off my cheeks. I pulled one, squeaking and squirming, from my hair. Pulled another one off my forehead.

I kicked my legs and swung my arms, frantically trying to free myself.

"Oww!" I let out a wild shriek as a fat, gray mouse scratched at my ear.

I reached up. Grabbed it. And squeezed.

The mouse gave a soft groan — and collapsed.

"Huh?" I felt something hard above its furry gray belly. Like a bump.

I slapped away two other mice and examined the one in my hand. I pushed the tiny, hard bump. The mouse started to squirm and struggle.

I pushed the bump again. The mouse slumped in my hand, silent and still.

"It's an on-off switch!" I screamed.

I turned to Marissa. She had fallen to her knees. Dozens of mice swarmed over her. They covered her sweatshirt. They crawled through her hair.

"It's an on–off switch!" I shouted to her. "Marissa — squeeze the button on their front. You can turn them off!"

I grabbed a mouse off my neck. Squeezed the button. Shut it off.

I swiped up two more and turned them off.

"They're not real!" I cried happily. "The mice — they're fakes! They're little machines!"

Marissa climbed to her feet. She was brushing mice off her clothes. Clicking them off. "Weird!" she exclaimed. "Justin — this is so weird!"

"We've got to get out of here," I told her. "We've got to find Luka."

Marissa tugged a mouse off the back of her neck and clicked it off. "Do you think this was the test?" she asked. "Do you think we passed it?"

"I don't know," I replied. My eyes searched the trees. "I don't care about the test right now. I just want to get away from these dumb mechanical mice."

I brushed two more off the front of my jeans. Then I reached for Marissa. I pulled a mouse off her shoulder, clicked it off, and tossed it away.

Then we both started to run for the trees.

Mice scurried under our feet. Their shrill squeaks echoed all around us.

We stepped on them as we ran. But we didn't care. We knew they weren't real. We knew they were mechanical.

We were nearly out of the clearing when I stopped suddenly. I had an idea.

I bent down and started scooping up mice. "Wait up!" I called to Marissa.

She didn't hear me. She kept running toward the trees.

"Wait up! I'll be right there!" I called. I picked up a few handfuls of mice and clicked them off. Then I shoved them into my backpack.

These will be *awesome* for playing jokes on people back home! I told myself. They're so lifelike. Can you imagine the fun I'll have with these in Miss Olsen's class?

I shoved eight or nine more of them into the pack and closed it up. Then I climbed to my feet and ran after my sister.

I glanced back once — and saw the mice, thousands of them, crawling over each other, crawling in wild circles through the grass.

Then I turned and ran, following Marissa into the safety of the white-trunked trees. Ran full-speed. Ran blindly.

So eager to get away from that clearing and the squeaking, scurrying mice.

"Marissa — wait up!" I called.

She was far ahead, running fast.

"Wait up!" I called.

And then I uttered a sharp cry as I ran — full-force — into a tree.

"Oooof!"

I felt the air burst from my lungs. I saw stars. Red and yellow stars, dancing in a pure white sky.

Gasping for breath, I reached for the tree trunk.

I heard a cracking sound.

So loud. And close.

The tree!

The tree I had run into — it started to fall!

"Look out — !" I called to my sister.

Too late.

As I stared helplessly, the tall, white tree collapsed.

Marissa's hands shot up as the tree fell on her.

And crushed her beneath its heavy trunk.

20

"Nooooo!" I let out a howl of horror. And stared down at my sister.

Marissa lay sprawled facedown in the dirt. The tree trunk had crushed her back and shoulders.

Was she breathing?

I couldn't tell.

"Marissa — !" I choked out her name and dropped down beside her. "I — I —"

I saw her body give a hard shake.

She raised her head and squinted up at me. "What happened?" Her words came out in a whisper.

"Does it hurt?" I cried. "Are you in pain?"

She squinted harder, as if thinking about it. "No. No pain." Marissa rolled onto her back. Then she reached up with both hands — and shoved the tree trunk off her.

"Huh?" I let out a startled cry.

I saw the bewildered expression on my sister's face. "It's fake too," she murmured.

She reached out and tugged off a chunk of the tree trunk. "It's plaster or something," she announced. "Check it out, Justin."

My hand was trembling as I tore off a piece of the trunk. I was still shaking all over from the sight of Marissa falling under the tree.

I squeezed the chunk of tree, and it turned to powder in my hand. I pulled off another hunk. Soft plaster.

Marissa climbed to her feet. She brushed the plaster dust off her clothes. "It's a total fake," she murmured again.

"Do you think the trees are *all* fake?" I cried. "The whole forest?"

I got up. Then I took a running start. Stuck both hands straight out in front of me . . .

. . . And ran as hard as I could, shoving my hands against a tree.

The trunk cracked easily. I stood shaking my head in amazement as the tree toppled over. It hit another tree and knocked that one down too. The plaster trunks cracked and shattered as they hit the ground.

"Fake. It's all a fake!" Marissa declared. A smile spread over her face. "That looks like fun."

She took a running start, aiming at a tree across from the others.

"No! Not that one!" I screamed.

I guess Marissa couldn't stop in time. She slammed her shoulder into the tree. "Yaaaay!"

She raised both fists over her head in triumph as the tree toppled over.

But she didn't have much time to cheer.

As the white trunk fell, I heard the hard flutter of wings.

And I watched in horror as dark forms fluttered up from the fallen limbs.

I had seen the bats. Dozens of black bats. Clinging upside down on the tree limbs.

I had seen them. But I hadn't warned Marissa in time.

And now the bats all came flapping up, chittering angrily, their sleep interrupted.

Hissing and shrieking at us, they surrounded us — and began to circle. I could feel the warm breeze from their flapping wings.

Faster. Faster, they circled.

"Are they fake too?" Marissa asked in a tiny voice.

"I — I don't think so," I stammered as they swooped in for the kill.

21

Marissa and I both ducked as the circle of bats swooped low.

I shut my eyes and covered my head with my hands.

And waited.

The sound of a deep *boom* rose over the shrill chittering of the bats.

The ground shook.

Thunder?

Another boom, low at first, then loud as an explosion.

I raised my head in time to see the white trees tremble.

The bats stopped their shrieking. Their wings shot up, stretched out.

Another boom of thunder sent them racing back up to the sky. I watched them flutter up, rising, rising above the trees, rising against the bright sky until they seemed to disappear into the sun.

Marissa let out a long sigh of relief. "We're safe." She climbed to her feet slowly.

"But what is that sound?" I demanded, listening hard.

Another thunderous *boom*. Closer this time.

I felt the ground shake. A tree tottered, then came toppling to the ground.

"It can't be thunder," Marissa said softly. She pointed to the sky. "No clouds or anything."

Another *boom*.

Closer.

"I — I know what it is," I stammered.

Marissa turned to me. Another *boom* shook the trees.

"Footsteps," I murmured. "Coming toward us. I know it's footsteps."

Marissa's mouth dropped open. "Justin — you're letting your crazy imagination run away with you. Again!"

"No. I'm right," I insisted. "Footsteps."

My sister squinted at me. "Are you losing it? What could make footsteps that loud? It would have to be . . ." Her voice trailed off.

Another *boom*.

I let my crazy imagination run away with me. I couldn't help it. I pictured a dinosaur. A Tyrannosaurus rex. Lumbering through the trees. Or maybe one of those fat ones with the long, skinny necks.

Booooooom. Booooom.

Or maybe *two* of them!

"Whatever it is, it's coming closer," Marissa whispered. She shook her head. "Ivanna *said* this was a test of survival. But —"

So far, it had been a test of our *running skills*!

But I didn't care. No way I wanted to stick around to see what this giant creature was.

As Marissa and I turned and started to run in the opposite direction, a shadow fell over us.

I gazed up to see if clouds had blocked the sun. But I saw no clouds overhead.

The shadow was cast by the creature, thundering closer and closer behind us.

I heard trees crunching underfoot. The ground shook. The heavy footsteps boomed close behind us.

How tall *was* it?

I glanced back — but could see only quivering trees.

Booooom. Booooom.

My knees buckled as the ground shook under my feet.

Marissa and I ran side by side. We hurtled through the trees as fast as we could, gasping for breath as we ran.

But we couldn't run out of the shadow. No matter how hard we ran, it floated over us, cold and dark.

Booooom. Booooom.

So close now. So close that every footstep made me leap into the air.

My heart thudded. My temples throbbed.

Marissa and I forced ourselves to keep running, desperate to escape, desperate to run out from under the wide shadow that seemed to hold us prisoner.

We ran until we reached a wide stream.

We both stopped inches from the muddy shore. And stared down into the fast-flowing, blue water.

"Now what?" I cried breathlessly. "Now what?"

The shadow darkened as the creature moved over us.

Marissa tugged my sleeve. "Look. You can see the bottom. It looks really shallow. Maybe we can walk across it. Or swim if we have to."

Boooom. Boooom.

The shadow darkened.

"Let's go," I said.

We stepped into the cold, clear stream.

22

The water flowed faster than I thought. I stepped onto the stream's soft bottom — and nearly lost my balance as the current swept around me.

I grabbed Marissa's shoulder to steady myself. We clung together for a moment, getting used to the water.

"Brrrr." I shivered. The water felt ice cold, even through my jeans legs.

But it was shallow, as Marissa had said. It came up only a few inches above my boots.

I took another step, leaning forward, trying to balance against the stream's fast current.

One more step. We were both halfway across the stream.

"Oh — !" I cried out when I realized I couldn't take the next step.

"Hey — !" Marissa exclaimed. I saw her struggling, too. "I'm stuck!"

"The bottom is so soft!" I cried. I worked to pull my foot up from the mud.

Stuck. My hiking boots had sunk below the surface of the muddy bottom.

I leaned down. And pulled. Pulled my leg up.

It wouldn't budge.

I grabbed my leg with both hands and tried to tug my foot out from the muddy stream bottom.

No.

"We—we're sinking!" Marissa wailed. "Justin — look! We're sinking fast!"

I swallowed hard. She was right. I could feel myself being pulled down. Down into the cold water, into the soft, sticky mud.

The water came up to my knees now. It seemed to be rising quickly.

But I knew the water wasn't going up. I was heading *down*.

"Pull off your boots and swim for it!" I instructed Marissa.

We both bent over and struggled to reach our hiking boots.

But they were buried too deeply in the mud.

The water rose up over my waist. If I kept sinking, it would be over my head in a few minutes.

Booom. Booom.

The thundering footsteps made the water ripple.

The dark shadow spread over the stream.

"Justin — look!" Marissa cried. She pointed to the other shore.

I turned to the shore — so close. But so far away.

I squinted into the shadows to see what she was gawking at. "What is it?" I cried.

"A big plug," Marissa reported. "In the stream bottom. Like a bathtub drain plug. This stream isn't real, either. It's a fake."

"The water feels plenty real!" I exclaimed, feeling myself sink even deeper into the mud. "Can you reach the plug, Marissa? Maybe if you pull it up, the water will drain."

She leaned toward it, bending at the waist. She stretched out both hands for the ring on top of the plug. "I–I'm trying," she groaned. "If only . . ."

Boooom. Booooom.

Marissa uttered a sigh. "I can't! I can't reach it! It's too far away."

The cold stream water flowed against my chest. I felt myself drop farther into the muddy bottom.

"I think we failed Ivanna's test," I murmured.

"Noooo!" Marissa wailed. She began thrashing at the water with both hands, twisting her body one way, then the other.

The deepening shadow moved over us.

I turned back and raised my eyes to the shore.

I saw the creatures lurching toward us.

And opened my mouth in an ear-shattering scream of horror.

23

At first I thought I was seeing black clouds, floating low over the trees.

But then I realized the bobbing shapes were too dark to be clouds. Too dark and too solid.

And then I saw the twin pairs of yellow eyes.

And I recognized the shapes of the heads. And I knew I was staring at cats.

Cats!

Black cats. Huge heads rising over the trees. Tails curling up like smoke from chimneys.

Two giant black cats, their paws thundering over the forest, shaking the ground and the trees. Their yellow eyes locked on Marissa and me.

"They're . . . not real!" Marissa murmured. "Not real . . . not real." She had stopped thrashing the water and stood now perfectly still, staring back at the enormous cats, repeating the words like a chant.

Trees crunched and fell. The two cats thundered their way to the shore.

"Noooo . . ." A low wail escaped Marissa's throat.

I struggled to breathe. My chest ached. My head started to spin.

The cats pulled back their lips in a terrifying hiss.

I saw rows of sharp teeth. I saw their yellow eyes narrow menacingly.

Tossing back their heads in another hiss, the creatures arched their backs. The black fur on their backs stood straight up.

"Wh-what are they going to do?" Marissa stammered.

I opened my mouth to answer her, but only a tiny squeak escaped.

The water flowed past my shoulders. I raised my hands out of the water, trying to keep from sinking under.

"Justin — what are they going to *do?*" she repeated in a shriek.

We didn't have to wait long to find out.

Before we could even cry out, the cat heads came swooping down at us. The jaws opened wide. The curled and jagged teeth slid apart.

I turned and tried to squirm and wriggle away. But I couldn't move. Water splashed over my face. Then I felt teeth clamp shut on the back of my sweatshirt.

Sputtering, gasping for breath, I felt myself

lifted up. My boots made a popping sound as they were pulled from the mud.

I felt the cat's hot breath on my neck and the back of my head. The teeth held me firmly, plucking me up, up out of the stream.

"Whoooooa!" I finally found my voice.

The cat dangled me high in the air.

My arms and legs thrashed wildly. The cat tossed its head, swinging me from side to side.

"Helllp! Ohhh, help!" I heard my sister's cry from nearby. I turned and saw her hoisted up by the other cat, hoisted high in the air, the cat's jaws clamped tightly on the back of Marissa's sweatshirt.

I tried to call out to Marissa. But a burst of hot cat breath nearly suffocated me.

I felt myself being lifted even higher as the cat rose up on its hind legs. A paw swung up and batted my side. The other paw batted me the other way.

Does it think I'm a cat toy? I wondered.

I didn't have time to think about it.

I twisted dizzily as the cat played with me, batting me from side to side. Then, suddenly, I found myself being lowered.

The jaws opened.

I was falling now.

Into the water?

No. I landed hard on my back on the shore. So hard, I bounced. Pain shot through my body.

I ignored it and scrambled to my feet. My heart pounding, my whole body shaking, I tried to run.

But the cat grabbed me up again, its jaws closing around my right shoulder.

As I sailed back up into the air, I saw Marissa falling through the air. I heard her cry out as she hit the ground. And then I saw the other black cat bend its head, open its jaws, and drag Marissa up in the air again.

Up — and then down. My body slammed hard on the shore. I gasped and struggled to my hands and knees. In time to be picked up again and dangled over the water.

Marissa and I both hung over the stream.

Then once more, we were dropped to the shore.

"Oww!" I bounced hard. Stared up as the cat lowered its massive head to pick me up again.

"What are they *doing*?" Marissa screeched. "Why are they *doing* this?"

"I know what they're doing. They're doing what cats always do!" I cried, feeling cold horror run down my body. "They're playing with their food."

24

"Whooooaaa!"

My stomach lurched as I felt myself being swooped up into the air again. A black cat's paw swiped at me and sent me swinging.

"They—they're going to *eat* us?" Marissa called.

"We must look like mice to them!" I shouted back.

And then I had an idea.

The cat tossed its head and sent me flying. It caught me between its enormous paws. The paws squeezed my middle so hard, I thought my head might pop off!

But as I struggled to breathe, my idea gave me hope.

Do I have time? I wondered. *Can I do it — before this cat swallows me whole?*

The cat tossed me up again, then caught me between its teeth. Pain shot down my back. My whole body tingled and ached.

With a groan, I twisted my body. I reached behind me and struggled to grab the backpack.

If I can unzip it, I thought, maybe I can reach the mechanical mice I stuffed inside. And maybe I can switch one or two of them on. And maybe the mice will distract the two cats. And maybe Marissa and I can escape.

Maybe, maybe, maybe.

But I *had* to try something. Or else, in a few seconds, Marissa and I would be cat chow.

The cat's tongue swept over the back of my neck. I cried out in pain. The tongue felt as rough as sandpaper! Hot cat breath stung my neck.

I grabbed the backpack with one hand and started to tug it around to my chest.

But the cat opened its jaws. The rough tongue bumped me from behind. And I went flying back to the ground.

I landed hard on my hands and knees. Pain shot through me once again. I felt like collapsing in the dirt.

But I knew I couldn't give up.

The cat leaned over me, hissing each breath. Yellow eyes gleamed down at me hungrily.

Ignoring the pain, I grabbed the backpack. I pulled the straps off my shoulder. Then I swung the pack around to my chest and gripped it tightly with both hands.

"Got to get the mice," I murmured out loud. "Got to get the kitty cat some mice to play with."

My hands were trembling so hard, I couldn't work the zipper.

"Aaaaagh!" I let out a frustrated cry — just as the cat swooped me up in its jaws again.

I tried to call out to Marissa. I wanted to tell her to hold on. That I had a plan.

High in the air, I gripped the backpack with my right hand. Reached for the zipper with my left.

Please. Please! I prayed silently. Let me get the mice out. Let me click them on.

"My only chance," I muttered, struggling with the backpack zipper. "My only chance . . ."

A burst of hot cat breath made me shudder. Once again I felt the dry, scratchy tongue scrape the back of my neck.

"Yessss!" I shouted as I finally pulled the zipper and opened the backpack.

"Yessss!"

I shot my hand excitedly into the backpack. I felt the furry mechanical creatures inside.

I started to wrap my fingers around one . . .

But the cat swung me hard. Tossed back its head and flung me into the air.

"Noooooo!" I let out a long wail — and felt the backpack fly out of my hands.

"Noooooo!" I frantically grabbed at it. Grabbed with both hands. Missed. Then I tried to snare it on my foot.

"Noooooo!" I watched the backpack sail to the ground.

It bounced once. Twice. Then lay in the dirt near the shore.

The cat caught me in its teeth. I felt the sharp points dig into my skin.

Then the jaws opened. And I started to slide. Down the scratchy tongue. Down, down into the cat's cavern of a mouth.

"Sorry, Marissa," I murmured in my panic. "We are doomed."

25

The ground disappeared from view as I slid further down the cat's rough tongue. On my stomach, I reached out with both hands.

And grabbed the two curved eyeteeth. They felt warm and sticky in my hands.

With a hard tug, I pulled myself part of the way up. I crawled a little way on the tongue. Then I gave another tug, and my head poked out from the cat's open mouth.

I searched for Marissa, but I couldn't see her.

Had she already been swallowed?

Beneath me, the tongue bucked and curled. The cat was trying to force me down.

But I held tightly onto the eyeteeth. And glimpsed the ground far below.

And saw three or four gray mice scampering out of the backpack, onto the dirt.

They must have clicked on when the backpack hit the ground!

Would the cats see them? Would they *care*?

The cat chomped its teeth together. I cried out in pain, and my hands slid off the eyeteeth.

The tongue rolled beneath me. I started to slide again.

The mouth closed over me, shutting me in darkness. "Ohhhh." So hot and wet inside. So hard to breathe.

I heard low gurgling and growling below me in the cat's stomach.

"No!" I cried. "No no no no!" My voice sounded tiny and muffled inside the cat's mouth.

And then, to my shock, the sunlight poured back in as the jaws popped open.

The tongue pushed me forward. Past the teeth. Past the lips.

I sucked in a deep breath of cool, fresh air.

And then I went flying from the cat's mouth.

I landed on my back on the ground next to Marissa. She gaped at me in surprise, her eyes wild, her red hair tangled and matted wetly to her head.

We both scrambled to our feet — in time to see both giant black cats pounce.

They both leaped at the same mechanical mouse.

Hissing and clawing at each other, they began to fight over it.

"Marissa — let's go!" I choked out.

She stared in amazement as the giant cats wrestled, hissing and scratching, rolling into the stream, then out again.

"Hurry! Let's go!" I shouted. I grabbed Marissa with both hands and tugged. "If they figure out the mice aren't real, they'll come back after us!"

"But are the *cats* real?" Marissa demanded, still gazing at them in amazement. "Are the cats real? Or fake?"

"*Who cares?*" I shrieked. "Let's get *out* of here!"

Once again, we started running through the forest. Which way were we headed? We didn't pay any attention. We just wanted to get as far away from those cats as we could.

My clothes felt wet and sticky from the inside of the cat's mouth. But the cool, fresh air felt good against my skin and helped to dry me off.

Our shadows leaned ahead of us, as if leading the way. I heard strange animal calls that sounded like shrill laughter. And I heard the flapping of wings above the trees.

But Marissa and I ignored all the sounds. We kept running, pushing tall weeds and shrubs out of our way, making our own path.

We didn't speak. We didn't even look at each other. We ran side by side, keeping each other in sight, helping each other through the tangled forest.

We were both breathless when we reached a round, grassy clearing. White and yellow moths floated silently over the swaying grass.

"Marissa — look!" I gasped, pointing to the other side of the clearing.

A small cabin stood under the trees where the grass ended. A very familiar cabin.

"It's Ivanna's!" Marissa exclaimed happily. "Justin — we made it! We're back!"

I sucked in a deep breath and scrambled across the grass. Marissa ran right behind me.

"Ivanna! Ivanna!" We both called her name as we hurried to the cabin.

She didn't come out. So I grabbed the door and pushed it open. "Ivanna — we're back!" I cried happily. I glanced quickly around the room, waiting for my eyes to adjust to the dim light.

Marissa pushed me aside as she burst into the small kitchen. "We survived!" she exclaimed. "Ivanna — is the test over? Did we pass it? Justin and I —"

We both saw Ivanna seated at the small wooden table. She sat stooped over, her head on the table.

Her horned helmet had fallen off. It lay on its side on the table. Her long blond braids had come undone and fallen over her face.

"Ivanna? Ivanna?" I called. I turned to my sister. "She must be asleep."

"Ivanna?" Marissa called. "We're back!"

The woman didn't stir.

I heard a whimper from the back of the room. Squinting into the shadows, I saw Silverdog. He was huddled sadly against the wall, his head on the floor between his paws. He let out another whimper.

"Justin — something is wrong here," Marissa whispered.

"Ivanna! Ivanna!" I shouted her name. But she still didn't move.

The big white dog whimpered sadly.

"Is she asleep?" Marissa demanded. "What's *wrong* with her?"

"Let's see," I murmured.

I took a deep breath and made my way across the kitchen to the table. Marissa raised her hands to her cheeks and stared at me. She didn't budge.

I was nearly to the table when I stopped with a gasp.

"Wh-what's wrong?" Marissa stammered.

"Look what's sticking out of her back!" I choked out.

26

"Huh?" Marissa's mouth dropped open in horror. "Justin — what?"

I swallowed hard. My legs started to tremble. I grabbed the back of a chair to steady myself.

"Marissa — look," I instructed, still pointing.

She came a couple of steps closer, her eyes bulging wide with fear.

We both stared at the metal object poking out from the back of Ivanna's dress.

A large metal key.

I worked up my courage and crept up behind Ivanna. My heart pounding, I leaned down and examined the big key.

"It–it's a *windup* key!" I stammered.

Marissa opened her mouth, but no sound came out.

I took the key in both hands and turned it one click.

Ivanna's head bobbed up, then fell back to the table.

"Yes. It's a windup key," I told my sister.

Ivanna's hands had drooped to the floor at her sides. I reached down and grabbed one of them.

It felt soft and spongy. Stuffed with cotton or something.

I let the hand drop to the floor and turned back to Marissa. "Ivanna isn't real," I told her, swallowing again. "She's some kind of dummy or puppet or something. Ivanna isn't real, either!"

"Then what *is* real?" Marissa demanded in a tiny voice. "This is so scary, Justin. Is it all part of a test, or what? How do we get out of here now? How do we find Dad? If Ivanna isn't real, then who is?"

I just shook my head. I didn't know how to answer her questions. I felt as frightened as she did.

My eyes fell on Silverdog back in the corner. The dog had his head buried in his paws. He whimpered softly.

Then, suddenly, the dog's ears perked up. He raised his head, his eyes flashing excitedly.

I heard a sharp growl behind me. From the door.

"Hey — !" I spun around as the door swung open.

And a growling, snarling creature burst in.

Luka!

His eyes moved hungrily from me to Marissa. A pleased grin spread over his wild face.

100

"No!" Marissa shrieked, backing away from him.

Luka tossed back his long hair with a shake of his head. He opened his mouth in a long howl.

He leaped into the center of the room. Tossed back his head in a roar. And hurtled toward us.

"Luka — stop!" I begged. "Don't hurt us!"

27

Luka's grin faded. He lowered his arms. He narrowed his dark eyes at me.

"I'm not going to hurt you," he said softly.

Marissa and I stared back at him in shock. "You — you can talk?" I stammered.

He nodded. "Yes. I can talk. And the first thing I want to say is, congratulations!" His smile returned.

He stepped across the room, walking upright like a human. He shook hands with Marissa, then with me. "Congratulations to both of you," Luka said warmly. "You passed the test."

"But — but —" I could only sputter.

Luka peeled a long strip of fur off his arm. Then he pulled the fur from around his neck. "I'm happy to get this stuff off," he said, peeling more fur from his arm. "It's so hot and itchy — especially when you're running around like a wild man in the forest."

"I'm very confused," I confessed.

Marissa nodded agreement. "Ivanna isn't real," she murmured. She motioned to Ivanna, slumped over the table behind us.

Luka shook his head. "No, she isn't. I built her myself. Just as I built all the creatures you found in my Fantasy Forest."

"But — why?" I choked out. "Why did you build all that?"

"As a test," Luka replied simply. He stepped up behind Ivanna and pulled her up into a sitting position. He brushed the dummy's hair behind her head with his hand. Then he propped the helmet back on her head.

"So many people come to the forest," Luka continued, turning back to Marissa and me. "They come searching for all kinds of treasures. Just as you two have.

"My family has lived in this forest for hundreds of years," Luka explained. "It became our job to protect many of the treasures. And so we built a test forest, to keep out those who were unworthy. To stop the people who don't deserve the wonderful treasures."

"You built the entire forest?" Marissa asked him.

He shook his head. "Just the part that isn't real."

"And how did we pass the test?" I demanded.

"By discovering what was real and what wasn't," Luka replied. "By surviving and triumphing over the unreal."

Marissa stared hard at Ivanna. The dummy's green eyes gazed dully back. "Why did you build Ivanna?" Marissa asked.

Luka grinned proudly. "She is my best creation. She keeps everyone from guessing that I am in charge here. No one believes that a wild wolf man runs the Fantasy Forest. It makes it so easy for me to watch everyone and see how they do on my test."

It all seemed very mysterious to me. But I was too happy it was all over to argue with him.

"And now I shall give you the treasure you came for," Luka announced. He turned quickly and disappeared into the back.

Marissa and I exchanged glances. "I can't believe it!" I whispered. "He's giving us the silver chest containing the Lost Legend! Dad is going to be so amazed!"

"We're going to be rich and famous!" Marissa exclaimed. "And Dad won't be able to tell us we're not helpful — ever again!"

A few seconds later, Luka returned carrying a small silver chest. "Congratulations again," he said solemnly. "I am happy to award you the ancient treasure that you came here to seek. And I wish you good fortune with it."

He placed the silver chest in my hands. It felt lighter than I expected. The silver gleamed in the light from the candle on the table.

My heart pounded. My hands trembled.

I suddenly felt so excited, I nearly dropped the silver chest! To think that I held the Lost Legend in my hands!

"Thank you," I managed to choke out.

"Yes, thank you," Marissa said. "Now how do we get back to our dad?"

Luka snapped his fingers. Back at the wall, Silverdog leaped to his feet.

"Silverdog will lead you back to your camp," Luka announced. "Stay close behind him, and he will protect you."

"Uh . . . protect us?" I asked, gripping the chest tightly.

Luka nodded. "There are many thieves in the forest. Some of them are real, and some of them are not real. But they all would steal your treasure and make it their own."

"We'll stay close to Silverdog," I promised.

We thanked Luka again. Then we followed the big white dog out of the cabin and back into the forest.

The afternoon sun had started to lower itself behind the trees. It cast an orange glow over the forest floor. The air had already begun to carry an evening chill.

Trotting steadily, the big dog kept his furry tail up high as he led the way, like a flag for us to follow. I carried the chest carefully between my hands and kept my eyes on the dog. Marissa followed close behind.

We walked along a curving path through a patch of tall yellow weeds. Then we made our way around a high clump of evergreen bushes.

On the other side of the bushes, Silverdog led us onto a leaf-covered path. Our boots crunched over the path as we hurried to keep up with the trotting dog.

I gripped the silver chest tightly. I couldn't wait to pull open the lid and gaze at the Lost Legend. To take it out and start to read it.

What was the legend about?

Who wrote it? And when was it written?

So many questions. And I knew they would all be answered as soon as we opened the chest and removed the legend from its hiding place of five hundred years.

The sun lowered itself behind the trees. Our shadows grew longer. The leaves crunched underfoot.

"Oh — wait!" I cried out when I heard leaves crunching behind us. "Wait —!"

Silverdog trotted on ahead of us.

But Marissa and I stopped.

And listened.

Listened to the crunching footsteps creeping up fast from the trees behind us.

I felt a chill of fear sweep down my back. "Marissa — we're being followed," I whispered.

28

"Luka warned us about thieves," Marissa whispered.

The crunching footsteps came closer. I tucked the silver chest under one arm as if protecting a football. My throat tightened. I could barely breathe.

I turned and saw Silverdog trotting on up ahead, his tail still raised behind him. The dog disappeared behind a clump of tall weeds.

"We can't just stand here," Marissa whispered.

The footsteps were approaching faster now. Any moment, I knew, some thief — or *several* thieves — would burst out of the trees and grab the chest away from us.

I turned to the tall weeds. I couldn't see the dog at all now.

"We have to run," Marissa whispered.

I listened to the crunching footsteps.

"We can't outrun him," I told her. "I can't run very fast. I have to be careful with this chest."

Marissa's blue eyes grew wide with panic. Then her expression changed. "I have an idea, Justin. Let's duck into those trees." She pointed. "The thief will run right past us. Then we'll hide there till he's out of sight."

Was it a good idea?

A terrible idea?

We had no time to think about it. We had to *move*.

We both spun around and started to run to the trees. *Toward* the approaching footsteps.

Would we make it to safety? Could we hide in the trees *before* he came rushing out at us?

I never found out.

About halfway across the grass, I tripped over a fallen tree limb.

"Ohhh!" I cried out.

And stumbled forward.

The silver chest flew from my hands.

"Noooooo!"

I desperately grabbed for it.

Missed.

Fell hard to my knees.

I watched the chest sail into the air.

And I stared in shock as a big man lumbered out of the dark shadows of the trees, raised his arms, and caught the chest easily.

29

I stared at the silver chest. Watched the man's hands pull it in, then hold it tightly.

Our chest.

Our Lost Legend.

We had gone through so many horrors to get it. And now someone else had taken it away.

I stared at the chest gripped so tightly in the man's hands. Then I raised my eyes to the man's bearded face.

"Dad!" I cried.

"Dad!" Marissa echoed. "I don't *believe* it!"

Beneath the beard, a grin spread quickly over Dad's face. "I don't believe it, either!" he cried. "Where have you been? Why did you run away? I've been searching the forest for you! Where were you?"

"It's kind of a long story," Marissa told him, rushing forward.

"Yes. Marissa and I have a legend of our own," I said.

Dad set the chest on the ground, and we both hugged him. Dad was so glad to see us, he had tears in his eyes. When we finished hugging, he hugged us both again.

"I can't believe I finally found you!" he exclaimed happily.

"And look what *we* found!" I declared, pointing to the chest.

Dad's mouth dropped open. When he jumped out and caught the chest, I don't think he realized what he had caught.

"It's — a silver chest!" he exclaimed.

"It's *the* silver chest!" I told him. "The silver chest we came to Brovania to find!"

"But — but — how?"

I never saw Dad so confused. Or so excited.

"The Legend of the Lost Legend," he murmured. He carefully lifted the chest off the ground. "This is the most thrilling moment of my life," he said. "How did you *do* this? How did you find this ancient chest? How did you — ?"

His voice cracked. I think he was too excited to speak.

"I told you, Dad. It's a very long story," I said.

"At least you can't say we weren't helpful!" Marissa chimed in.

All three of us laughed.

"Do you realize what this will mean to us?" Dad asked, lowering his voice to a whisper. "Do you realize what a thrilling discovery this is?"

He dropped down to his knees to admire the chest. He tenderly ran his hands over the smooth silver of the lid.

"Beautiful. Beautiful," he repeated, grinning.

"Can we open it?" Marissa asked, dropping down on the ground beside him. "Please, Dad? Can we open it and see the Lost Legend?"

"We *have* to see it!" I exclaimed eagerly. "We *have* to!"

Dad nodded. "Yes. We *have* to!" He laughed. "Believe me, I'm even more impatient to see it than you two are!"

He bent over the chest. I saw his hands tremble as he lowered them to the silver clasp.

"Beautiful. Beautiful," he murmured again.

His hands closed around the clasp. He turned it, then gave a sharp tug.

Slowly, slowly, he pulled open the lid.

And all three of us leaned close and gazed into the chest.

30

We leaned so close over the chest, our heads touched.

"I — I don't *believe* it!" I gasped.

"What *is* it?" Marissa shrieked.

Dad's mouth dropped open. He narrowed his eyes and gazed into the chest. He didn't say a word.

"It–it's an *egg!*" I finally stammered.

The three of us were staring down at a large yellow egg with brown speckles.

"But — where is the Lost Legend?" Marissa demanded. "This can't be it!"

Dad sighed and shook his head. "This isn't the right silver chest," he said softly.

He reached inside and carefully lifted the egg. Then he felt around on the bottom of the chest with his free hand. "Nothing else in here. Just an egg."

He examined the egg, rolling it slowly between

his hands. Then he carefully lowered it back into the chest. "Just an egg," he repeated sadly.

I let out a hoarse cry. "But Marissa and I passed the test!" I wailed. "Luka said he would give us what we came here for!"

"Who is Luka?" Dad asked. He carefully closed the clasp on the chest. Then, with a groan, he climbed to his feet. "Where can we find him?"

Before I could answer, I heard a rustling sound across the clearing. I turned to see Silverdog come trotting out of the weeds.

"Silverdog!" I cried. I rushed forward and petted the dog's big head and the fur around his neck. "Take us back to Luka!" I ordered him. "Luka! Take us to Luka!"

Silverdog wagged his tail. Did that mean he understood?

"Luka!" I repeated. "Take us to Luka!"

Still wagging his bushy tail, the big dog headed past us to the trees. Dad picked up the silver chest. And the three of us followed the dog back through the forest.

Marissa and I hadn't traveled far from the little cabin. A few minutes later, it came into view. Luka hurried out, his face twisted in surprise.

"I didn't expect to see you back here," he said, shaking out his long, dark hair. "Did you get lost?"

"No. Not exactly," Marissa replied.

"This is our dad," I told Luka. "We finally found him."

Dad and Luka shook hands.

"Well, why did you come back here?" Luka demanded. He lowered his gaze to the silver chest in Dad's hands. "I gave you what you came here for."

"Not exactly," Dad replied. "It's an egg."

"Yes, I know," Luka said, scratching his jaw.

"But we didn't come here for an egg!" I protested.

Luka narrowed his eyes at us. "You didn't come to the forest in search of the Eternal Egg of Truth?"

"No way," I replied. "Dad brought us here to find the Legend of the Lost Legend."

"Oops!" Luka blushed. "I made a little goof." He looked very upset.

"That's okay," Dad said softly. "Everyone makes mistakes."

Luka shook his head. "I'm so sorry. I usually get it right. I really thought you were searching for the Eternal Egg of Truth."

Still shaking his head, he took the silver chest from Dad's hands. He carried it into the cabin. A few seconds later, he returned. "A thousand apologies," he said.

"But can you help us find the Lost Legend?" I demanded. "Do you have it?"

"Do I have it?" The question seemed to surprise Luka. "No. I don't have it. I think it will be very hard to get it."

"Why?" Dad asked eagerly. "Do you know where it is?"

Luka nodded. "Yes. I can direct you to the people who have the Lost Legend. But I do not think they will part with it. They have been wandering the forest with it for five hundred years. I do not think they will want to give it to you — for any price."

"I — I just want to talk with them!" Dad cried excitedly. "I just want to *see* it with my own eyes!"

"Go in this direction," Luka instructed us, pointing. "Cross two streams, and you will probably find them on a wide, stone clearing. They wander the forest. They never stay in the same place for long. But I think you will find them in the stone clearing if you hurry."

"Thank you!" Dad cried, shaking Luka's hand.

We all thanked Luka. Then we hurried off in the direction he had pointed. We were so excited, all three of us talked at the same time.

"Do you think they'll be friendly?"

"Do you think they'll let us see the Lost Legend?"

"Do you think they'll let me borrow it?" Dad asked. "If I could only borrow it for a few weeks. . . ."

"Luka said they might not be friendly."

"He said they might not part with it — for any price."

The journey across the two streams was not difficult. We walked for only an hour.

We were still talking excitedly as we drew near their camp. We stopped on a low hill overlooking a wide patch of stony ground.

The stone clearing.

We could see rows of small tents made of animal hides. Several people, dressed in brown robes, worked to build a fire in the center of the clearing. A bunch of scrawny gray dogs wrestled and snapped at each other at the edge of the clearing.

"I can't believe it," Dad exclaimed, his eyes searching the small tent village. "I can't believe these wanderers actually *have* the Lost Legend."

"But will they let us *see* it?" I asked.

"Only one way to find out," Dad replied. He led the way down the hill. "Hello, there!" he called out to the wanderers. "Hello!"

31

"Hello, there! Hello!"

As we stepped onto the stone ground, the scrawny gray dogs stopped wrestling. Barking furiously, they came scurrying up to greet us. They lowered their heads, bared their jagged teeth, and growled.

Marissa, Dad, and I stopped. I saw three men in brown robes come running out of tents. They quickly shooed the dogs away. The men, I saw, were as scrawny as the dogs.

"Hello," Dad greeted them warmly. "I am Professor Richard Clarke, and this is Justin and Marissa."

The three men nodded solemnly. But they did not speak.

Two of them were bald. One had long, wavy white hair and a bushy white mustache.

Marissa and I exchanged glances.

I could see that she was as frightened as I was.

These brown-robed wanderers did *not* look friendly.

The white-haired man spoke first. "How did you find us?" he demanded coldly.

"Someone directed us to you," Dad replied.

"Why have you come here, Professor Clarke?" the wanderer asked.

"We're searching for the Legend of the Lost Legend," Dad told him.

The three men all gasped in shock. They leaned close and whispered furiously to each other.

When they finished their excited conversation, they turned back to us. But they didn't speak.

"Do you have it?" Dad asked eagerly. "Do you have the Lost Legend?"

"Yes," the white-haired man replied. "Yes, we have it."

He whispered something to the two bald men. They spun around, their long robes twirling with them, and hurried away.

A few seconds later, they returned. One of them carried a small silver chest.

"Oh, my goodness!" Dad declared, his eyes bulging. "Is that it? Is that really it? Is that the Lost Legend?"

"Yes," the white-haired man replied. "Do you want it?"

"Huh?" all three of us cried.

The wanderer shoved the chest into my hands. I was so shocked, I nearly dropped it!

"It is yours," the white-haired man said. He stepped back.

Dad swallowed hard. "Are you *sure*?" he cried. "Are you sure you want to give it to us?"

"Yes. Take it," the man replied quickly. "Good-bye."

He and the other two turned and walked quickly back to their tents. To our surprise, they instantly began to pack up.

Dozens of wanderers began pulling up tents, packing up supplies, putting out the campfire. In minutes, they had scurried away.

The stone clearing stood bare. No sign they had ever been there.

"How strange," Dad said. "How totally strange."

We began to walk away from the clearing. I think all three of us were in shock or something. I know I was completely stunned.

"They handed the treasure over to us without a word," Dad said, rubbing his beard. "Why did they *do* that? Why did they give this treasure to us without asking for anything in return? I just can't believe it."

I still had the chest in my arms. After we had walked for a short while, I stopped. "Where are we going?" I demanded. "Let's open the chest. Let's take a look at it!"

"Yes!" Dad agreed. "I am so surprised — so stunned — I guess I don't know what I'm doing!"

He took the chest from me and carefully set it down on the ground. "Let's see it. Let's finally see it!"

Carefully, he unlatched the lid and opened the chest. Then he reached inside — and pulled out a manuscript. A thick stack of yellowed paper with tiny black writing all over it.

"Yes!" Dad whispered happily. "Yes!"

He gripped the ancient legend tightly in both hands and held it down so that Marissa and I could see it.

"Wow!" Marissa cried. "It really looks five hundred years old — doesn't it?"

"Dad, what does it say on the top page?" I asked, struggling to make out the words.

"Uh . . . let's see," Dad replied. He raised the manuscript close to his face, squinted hard at the tiny words, and then read them out loud:

"WHOEVER OWNS THE LOST LEGEND WILL BE LOST FOREVER."

"Huh? What does *that* mean?" I cried.

Dad shrugged. "It doesn't really mean anything. It's just part of the legend."

"Are you sure?" Marissa demanded in a trembling voice.

Dad stared down at the manuscript. " 'Lost forever . . .' " he murmured. " *'Whoever owns the Lost Legend will be lost forever.'* "

Then he raised his eyes to the trees that surrounded us. "Hey — where are we?"

All three of us gazed around at the strange, dark trees.

We had wandered away from the stone clearing. Now nothing looked familiar.

"Where are we?" Dad repeated.

"We—we're lost," I whispered.

About R.L. Stine

R.L. STINE is the most popular author in America. He is the creator of the *Goosebumps*, *Give Yourself Goosebumps*, *Fear Street*, and *Ghosts of Fear Street* series among other popular books. He has written more than 100 scary novels for kids.

Bob lives in New York with his wife, Jane, and teenage son, Matt.

Add *more*

Goosebumps®

to your collection . . .
A chilling preview of
what's next from
R.L. STINE

ATTACK OF THE
JACK-O'-LANTERNS

9

"I want to trick-or-treat all night!" Walker exclaimed. "This may be our last trick-or-treat night ever."

"Excuse me? What do you mean?" Tabby demanded, turning her green face to him.

"Next year, we'll be teenagers," Walker explained. "We'll be too old to trick-or-treat."

Kind of a sad thought.

I tried to take a deep breath of cool air. But I had forgotten to cut a nose or mouth hole in the sheet. We hadn't even left my front yard, and I was already starting to feel hot inside it!

"Let's start at The Willows," I suggested.

The Willows is a neighborhood of small houses. It starts on the other side of a small woods, just two blocks away.

"Why The Willows?" Tabby demanded, fiddling with her tiara.

"Because the houses are real close together," I told her. "We don't have to walk much, and we'll get a lot of candy. No long driveways to walk up and down."

"Sounds good," Lee agreed.

We started walking along the curb. Across the street, I saw two monsters and a skeleton making their way across a front yard. Little kids, followed by a father.

The wind fluttered my costume as we walked. My shoes crunched over frost-covered dead leaves. The sky seemed to grow darker as we made our way past the bare black trees of the woods.

A few minutes later, we reached the first block of The Willows. Streetlights cast a warm yellow glow over the neighborhood. A lot of the houses were decorated with orange and green lights, cutouts of witches and goblins, and flickering jacko'-lanterns.

The four of us began walking from house to house, gleefully yelling "Trick or treat!" and collecting all kinds of candy.

People oohed and aahed over Tabby's princess costume. She was the only one in our group who had bothered to put on a decent costume. So I guess she stood out.

We passed by a lot of other kids as we made our way down the block. Most of them appeared younger than us. One kid was dressed as a milk carton. He even had all the nutritional information printed on one side.

It took us about half an hour to do both sides of the street. The Willows ended at a traffic circle. Kind of a dead end.

"Where to next?" Tabby asked.

"Whoa. Wait. One more house," Walker said. He pointed to a small brick house set back in the trees.

"I didn't see that one," I said. "I guess because it's the only house that isn't right on the street."

"The lights are on, and they've got a pumpkin in the window," Walker announced. "Let's check it out."

We trooped up to the front stoop and pushed the doorbell. The front door swung open instantly. A small, white-haired woman poked out her head. She squinted through thick eyeglasses at us.

"Trick or treat!" the four of us chanted.

"Oh, my goodness!" she exclaimed. She pressed wrinkled hands against her cheeks. "What wonderful costumes!"

Huh? Wonderful costumes? I thought. Two bedsheets and a borrowed Superman suit from last year?

The old woman turned back into the house. "Forrest, come see this!" she called. "You've got to see these costumes."

I heard a man cough from somewhere deep inside the house.

"Come in. Please come in," the old woman

pleaded. "I want my husband to see you." She stepped back to make room for us to enter.

The four of us hesitated.

"Come in!" she insisted. "Forrest has to see your costumes. But it's hard for him to get up. Please!"

Tabby led the way into the house. We stepped into a tiny, dimly lit living room. A fire blazed in a small brick fireplace against one wall. The room felt like a blast furnace. It had to be five hundred degrees in there!

The woman shut the front door behind us. "Forrest! Forrest!" she called. She turned to us and smiled. "He's in the back room. Follow me."

She opened the door and let us enter. To my surprise, the back room was enormous.

And jammed with kids in costumes.

"Whoa!" I cried out, startled. My eyes quickly swept the room.

Most of the kids had taken off their masks. Some of them were crying. Some were red-faced and angry. Several kids sat cross-legged on the floor, their expressions glum.

"What's going on?" Tabby demanded shrilly. Her eyes bulged wide with fear.

"What are they all doing here?" Lee asked, swallowing hard.

A red-faced little man with shaggy white hair came hobbling out from the corner, leaning on a white cane. "I like your costumes," he said, grinning at us.

"We — we have to go now," Tabby stammered.

We all turned to the door. The old woman had shut it behind her.

I glanced back at the kids in costumes. There were at least two dozen of them. They all looked so frightened and unhappy.

"We have to go," Tabby repeated shrilly.

"Yeah. Let us out of here," Lee insisted.

The old man smiled. The woman stepped up beside him. "You have to stay," she said. "We like to look at your costumes."

"You can't go," the man added, leaning heavily on his cane. "We have to look at your costumes."

"Huh? What are you *saying*? How long are you going to keep us here?" Tabby cried.

"Forever," the old couple replied in unison.

GET
Goosebumps®
by R.L. Stine

❏ BAB62836-4	Tales to Give You Goosebumps	
	Book & Light Set Special Edition #1	$11.95
❏ BAB26603-9	More Tales to Give You Goosebumps	
	Book & Light Set Special Edition #2	$11.95
❏ BAB74150-4	Even More Tales to Give You Goosebumps	$14.99
	Book and Boxer Shorts Pack Special Edition #3	

———————————— GIVE YOURSELF GOOSEBUMPS ————————————

❏ BAB55323-2	Give Yourself Goosebumps #1:	
	Escape from the Carnival of Horrors	$3.99
❏ BAB56645-8	Give Yourself Goosebumps #2:	
	Tick Tock, You're Dead	$3.99
❏ BAB56646-6	Give Yourself Goosebumps #3:	
	Trapped in Bat Wing Hall	$3.99
❏ BAB67318-1	Give Yourself Goosebumps #4:	
	The Deadly Experiments of Dr. Eeek	$3.99
❏ BAB67319-X	Give Yourself Goosebumps #5:	
	Night in Werewolf Woods	$3.99
❏ BAB67320-3	Give Yourself Goosebumps #6:	
	Beware of the Purple Peanut Butter	$3.99
❏ BAB67321-1	Give Yourself Goosebumps #7:	
	Under the Magician's Spell	$3.99
❏ BAB84765-1	Give Yourself Goosebumps #8:	
	The Curse of the Creeping Coffin	$3.99
❏ BAB84766-X	Give Yourself Goosebumps #9:	
	The Knight in Screaming Armor	$3.99
❏ BAB53770-9	The Goosebumps Monster Blood Pack	$11.95
❏ BAB50995-0	The Goosebumps Monster Edition #1	$12.95
❏ BAB60265-9	Goosebumps Official Collector's Caps	
	Collecting Kit	$5.99
❏ BAB73906-9	Goosebumps Postcard Book	$7.95
❏ BAB73902-6	The 1997 Goosebumps 365 Scare-a-Day Calendar	$8.95
❏ BAB73907-7	The Goosebumps 1997 Wall Calendar	$10.99

- -

Scare me, thrill me, mail me GOOSEBUMPS now!

Available wherever you buy books, or use this order form. Scholastic Inc., P.O. Box 7502,
2931 East McCarty Street, Jefferson City, MO 65102

Please send me the books I have checked above. I am enclosing $_____ (please add
$2.00 to cover shipping and handling). Send check or money order—no cash or C.O.D.s please.

Name _____Age _____

Address _____

City_____State/Zip _____

Please allow four to six weeks for delivery. Offer good in the U.S. only. Sorry, mail orders are not available to
residents of Canada. Prices subject to change.

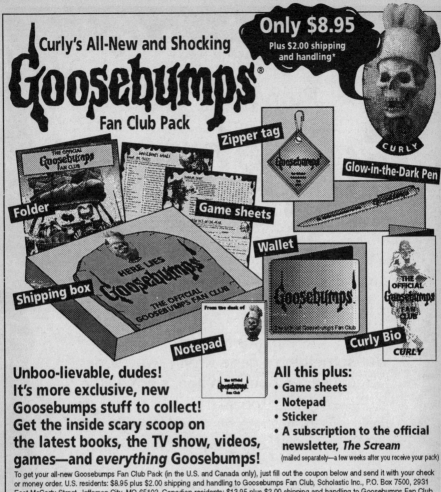

Pumpkin Power!

Goosebumps®

Nothing beats Halloween. And Drew and her best friend, Walker, have planned the perfect Halloween prank. Two of their friends are even dressing up as pumpkin heads to help.

But something's gone wrong. Way wrong. Because the pumpkin heads are a little too scary.

With strange hissing voices.

And flames shooting out of their faces....

ATTACK OF THE JACK-O'-LANTERNS

Goosebumps #48
by R.L. Stine

Coming soon to a bookstore near you!

R.L. STINE
GIVE YOURSELF
Goosebumps®

He's One Mad Mummy!

You're on vacation with your family when you decide to check out a cool exhibit of Egyptian artifacts that includes an actual mummy! But this is no ordinary artifact—this mummy wants out. And that's just what he gets!

Now you must find him. Search the museum and uncover a secret diary that gives clues to his location. Or set out after him on your own— but watch out! If you touch his bandages you turn into a mummy, too! Will you get your own body back before time runs out?

Give Yourself Goosebumps #10
Diary of a Mad Mummy
by R.L. Stine

Coming soon to a bookstore near you!

It's Every
Dummy's Dream!

Slappy's eyes really light up!

Goosebumps®

*Three books in one! Surprise!
An awesome cover with flashing eyes!*
Get three of your all-time favorite stories:
*Night of the Living Dummy #7,
Night of the Living Dummy II #31,* and
Night of the Living Dummy III #40—
together in *one* hardcover book that
lights up when
you open it!

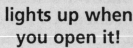

The Goosebumps Monster Edition #2

by R.L. Stine

Coming to a bookstore near you!